Sugar Spinett's Little Instruction Book

Now, there's a book I wouldn't want to judge by the cover. What that Mase Lebow is doing at this bachelor auction I couldn't tell you. First of all, the man looks plain dangerous, that's what. Attractive, but dangerous. And the brochure says he's a cop, for heaven's sake. *I* wouldn't feel safe with him.

And then, he's got a child with him. And that little boy looks as uncomfortable as his father. They're going to lose money on this contender, I'm sure. Who would bid on him? Someone looking for trouble?

Dear Reader,

We just knew you wouldn't want to miss the news event that has all of Wyoming abuzz! There's a herd of eligible bachelors on their way to Lightning Creek—and they're all for sale!

Cowboy, park ranger, rancher, P.I.—they all grew up at Lost Springs Ranch, and every one of these mavericks has his price, so long as the money's going to help keep Lost Springs afloat.

The auction is about to begin! Young and old, every woman in the state wants in on the action, so pony up some cash and join the fun. The man of your dreams might just be up for grabs!

Marsha Zinberg
Editorial Coordinator, HEART OF THE WEST

Courting Callie
Lynn
Erickson

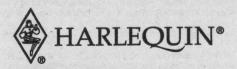

TORONTO • NEW YORK • LONDON
AMSTERDAM • PARIS • SYDNEY • HAMBURG
STOCKHOLM • ATHENS • TOKYO • MILAN • MADRID
PRAGUE • WARSAW • BUDAPEST • AUCKLAND

Lynn Erickson is acknowledged as the author
of this work.

ISBN 0-373-82586-2

COURTING CALLIE

Copyright © 1999 by Harlequin Books S.A.

Visit us at www.romance.net

Printed in U.S.A.

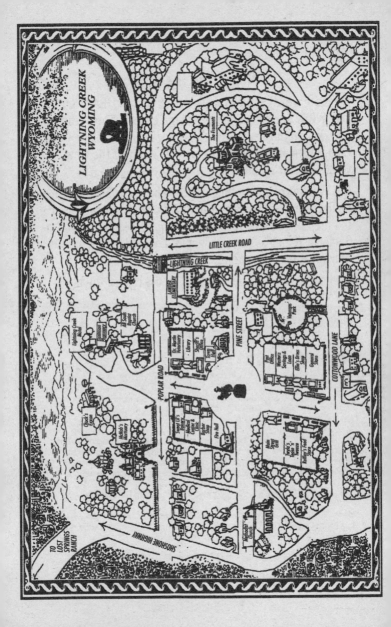

A Note from the Author

When we were asked to write a book for the HEART OF THE WEST series, we jumped at the chance. The setting was right in our backyard—Wyoming is next door to Colorado—and we love to share the vistas of the New West with our readers.

But even more compelling was the chance to demonstrate equine therapy's large and small miracles. Carla attended the therapy sessions of a local group, and each one of the Someday Ranch's "guests" inspired our story. The horses, of course, play themselves.

We hope you enjoy the story and all the rest of the books to follow in the series.

Sincerely,

Carla and Molly
The Lynn Erickson team

This book is dedicated to all the equine therapists who perform their miracles with compassion and patience every day of the year.

CHAPTER ONE

CALLIE THORNE HAD no idea she was muttering aloud to herself until her friend strolled up.

"Hey, Callie," Lindsay said, "it can't be that bad. Look around you. Everyone's having a ball."

Callie let out a whistling breath. It was true. Everyone at the Lost Springs Ranch for Boys was having a rousing good time. There must have been a hundred people—men, women and children—gathered around the showring where the much-anticipated bachelor auction was soon to get under way. Dogs were running loose, and boys from the ranch raced around, creating chaos. Their counselors were trying to keep them in some kind of order, but it was a weekend, the atmosphere festive, and their efforts proved futile.

The crowd wasn't all from nearby Lightning Creek, Wyoming. People had come from as far away as New York and Los Angeles for the auction. There was a bevy of handsome men to bid on—a whole catalog full of them. Each one had his picture in the glossy brochure, along with a brief profile listing likes and dislikes, favorite song, most embarrassing moment.... One photo showed a good-looking guy in a tuxedo with a rose in his hand, another in a chef's hat and apron.

Most of the bachelors were success stories, graduates of this very ranch, where troubled boys often found a new path in life. Callie had read all about them. The brochure was still in her back pocket. The auction was a worthy event, designed to raise money for the ranch, which was facing financial difficulties. Callie couldn't have been happier about the super turnout. Her friend Lindsay Duncan's family had owned and operated the place for many years, and now Lindsay owned it. Proceeds from the auction would help put the ranch back on its feet.

Callie only wished she hadn't agreed to participate. Suddenly, a fantasy image popped into her head. She was used to these dreamscapes by now, though she never confided about them to anyone. They came to her at the strangest times, often right in the middle of a totally unrelated situation, and while she watched the scene play out in her mind, she knew she must look unfocused, as if she were daydreaming. Probably that was why people thought of her as a bit of a…crackpot. In this fantasy, she bid on a great-looking bachelor— actually won him for a weekend date. He was everything a woman could dream of: handsome, intelligent, kind and sympathetic, with a smile that made her legs go all watery. He was rich. They were camping out. Sure, Callie thought, why not? Camping beneath a heavenly black velvet sky right on her own ranch. A big steak sizzling in an iron frying pan, and propped up against a rock was an opened bottle of wine. Firelight danced in the man's eyes, and he was leaning close to Callie, telling her this bachelor date was the best thing that had ever happened to him. His lips— the most sensual lips she'd ever seen on a man—parted to kiss her. Her heart sang.… And then he confessed there was this one little thing he had to tell her. He was, uh, married, but it was a bad marriage, and he was miserable.…

Callie blinked away the image and realized Lindsay was looking at her curiously. "Let's just forget about the auction part, Lindsay. I'll write you a check, a donation. I don't have to bid on anyone, really. I'd be happy to just contribute…"

"No way," Lindsay said emphatically, shaking her head. "You never get off your ranch. This'll do you a world of good."

"*I* never get out?" Callie protested. "I'm with people twenty-four hours a day. I'm perfectly happy—"

"Yes, with your work," Lindsay said, interrupting. "But you could use a date. You know? A guy? A *date?*"

Every time Callie had gotten hooked up with a man in the last ten years it had been disastrous. She always fell for the losers, the stray puppy-dog types.

"Now, look at that guy over there, the one near Rex…" Lindsay nodded across the showring to where Rex Trowbridge, local lawyer and director of the ranch, was standing with Lindsay's uncle Sam Duncan, a retired counselor. They were talking to one of the men about to be auctioned off. "He's a park ranger from Yellowstone. Zeke is his name. I even remember him from when he was one of our problem kids. He turned himself around, has a great life as a ranger, and he's very available.…"

Callie shook her head emphatically. "I just can't. I can't go through with this auction stuff." Even as she spoke, the auctioneer was testing the microphone in the middle of the dusty showring, pinging the mike with a finger, and people were already beginning to cheer and whistle, anticipating the first man to go on the block. "I feel…sick," Callie said, aware of a warm flush spreading across her cheeks.

Someone called out to Lindsay then, and she gave Callie an apologetic smile and turned to leave. "I'll be back," she said. "I've got to socialize. Just keep checking out the guys. You'll find someone."

Callie stood digging a pointy-toed cowboy boot into the dust, her head down, eyes covered by the brim of her well-worn Stetson, hands jammed into her jeans pockets. She told herself she could do this. It was for Lindsay and her uncle Sam, and all the boys would benefit. But, wow, she wished it were over. It was just too, well, embarrassing. *Buying* a man.

While the women took their seats in the grandstand, Callie made a beeline for the ranch house and the ladies' room. Maybe she could hide inside till it was all over, say she'd gotten sick, write Lindsay that check. That's what she'd do, all right. Hide out. *Chicken* out.

She passed Twyla, who owned the beauty parlor in Lightning Creek. Callie considered stopping to talk, but Twyla was busy selling raffle tickets on a quilt made by women in the local hospital guild.

When she reached the ranch house, the bathroom had an endless line, and she really didn't need to use it, anyway. She wandered aimlessly around the place, eyeing the elk antlers on the walls, the river-rock fire-place and Navajo rugs, as if this were the first time she'd been to Lost Springs Ranch.

People were milling everywhere. Inside and out. Around the bunkhouse dorms, crowding the barbecue pit, from which rose the delicious aromas of ribs and chicken cooking on spits. There were tables laden with food: coleslaw, potato salad, corn on the cob, baked beans, brownies and corn bread. Ice-filled wooden tubs held bottles of soda and beer. But all Callie could see was that great big beautiful guy by her imaginary campfire. Married.

Callie stood off to the side beneath a cottonwood tree and watched as the first man climbed onto the block and made a mock bow to the assembled throng. The women cheered and yelled out catcalls as the auctioneer gave a brief introduction, then began his singsong litany. "Who'll give me five hundred dollars? I have five. Who'll bid six? I have six six six, seven. Who'll give me eight eight, nine."

Callie watched the whole thing in mute fascination. The bachelor was trying to bump up the bids with a big flashy smile toward the grandstand, where the women egged him on. Once he even posed, flexing his biceps—Mr. Universe. Everyone loved it, and the air was split with whistles. The bidding went on under the hot June sun. "I have eighteen, who'll give me nineteen? Nineteen nineteen nineteen. Nineteen! Who'll give me two thousand, two two."

Callie wished she felt more like participating. The auction was for a wonderful cause, the proof of which was in the men being bid on. Alumni of Lost Springs, they'd turned their lives around, thanks to the ranch. And there were so many boys like them here today. It was just that she had so little free time. Her ranch, an equine therapy ranch five miles up the road, kept her so busy that months seemed to fly by like days. She didn't have time for a date—even one she paid for.

Callie tipped the brim of her Stetson back, looked up at the pellucid Wyoming sky and sighed. *Write a check and hightail it out of here,* she mused. *Just do it.*

Then she thought about all the folks back at her ranch, her parents, her assistant, the cook and the housemother who tended to the therapy guests. They'd all stood out in the drive this morning, eyed her new jeans and western-cut blue-and-white-checked shirt and her favorite Stetson, and told her to go get herself a good one. Her father, Tom Thorne, had even called out for her to bid as high as she wanted on a nice young man. "It's for a great cause," he'd said.

Well, she knew there were definite limits to the amount she could spend despite what her dad had said. Their ranch was doing okay. But just okay. And, like Lost Springs, the Someday Ranch depended on a lot of volunteer help from the neighboring town of Lightning Creek. Maybe this commitment she had made to Lindsay and the auction wasn't such a good idea after all. Maybe...

"I found him" came a voice at her ear, startling her. It was Lindsay. "I found you just the right bachelor. Come on."

Before Callie could protest, Lindsay had her by the arm and was dragging her toward a barn behind the grandstand. "Quit it, Lindsay," Callie was saying, and that was when she saw the man.

She stopped short, about thirty yards from where he was standing, talking to another guy. Her breath caught.

"Pretty nice on the old eyes, huh?" Lindsay whispered, and she nudged Callie in the ribs.

"Uh..." was all Callie got out.

He *was* something to look at. About six feet tall, lean and fit. He had a full head of wavy dark hair with a lock that escaped and lay curled on his forehead. And a mustache. A great thick mustache over full lips. Even from where Callie stood gaping, she could see the blue of his eyes—like the blue of the Wyoming sky.

A city boy, Callie was thinking when Lindsay told her he was a cop. "He's from Colorado. Denver," she said, and Callie recalled noticing him in the brochure. But now, in the flesh, she could see the alertness in him. It was in the pitch of his head, the flex of his knee beneath the tan Dockers, the tension in his square jaw. A cop.

Then, abruptly, as if he sensed the two pairs of eyes on him, the man pivoted and glared at them. Lindsay giggled. But Callie wasn't laughing. Despite the heat of the summer day, a chill ran up her spine. He looked downright menacing.

"Good grief," she whispered, shifting her gaze away. "What's with him?"

Lindsay shrugged. "Haven't a clue. I don't remember him that well from the ranch. His name's Mason LeBow. He goes by Mase. I think he was married."

"Was?" Callie asked.

"I guess. I really don't remember." Suddenly Callie saw a little boy, maybe six or seven years old, run up to this Mase LeBow and grab onto his pant leg, cowering behind him. The man, Mase, reached down and patted the child's head and gave him a smile, one that didn't quite reach those glacial-blue eyes. He looked so out of sync in this happy crowd, and for the life of her, Callie had no idea why he would elicit such an uncharacteristic response in her.

She stole another glance at the cop. Dangerous. That was all she could think. He looked dangerous. And she knew suddenly that Lindsay had found the perfect bachelor for her to bid on. Who would want a date with this guy? She'd bet she could buy him for a song and a dance, too. And even better, Callie wouldn't have to go through with the date. She'd let him off the hook immediately, tell him whatever came to mind.

The only thing that stirred Callie, that tweaked her curiosity, was the little boy. He looked enough like Mase LeBow to be his son. Probably was. Callie couldn't imagine the man agreeing to a "bachelor" date if he were married. So he must be divorced. And the wife, ex-wife, couldn't take the kid for the weekend, and Mase got stuck with him. Maybe that was why he was looking so uncomfortable. The child, too. The poor boy was feeling his father's tension, responding to those bad vibes. How awful, Callie thought. She'd bid on this man for sure and immediately set him free from any obligation. Everyone would go home happy. *Perfect,* she thought.

But when it was Mase LeBow's turn on the block, Callie froze.

To begin with, the bidding was slow. It was that look on the cop's face. Oh, he was trying to cloak it, but still the jaw was tight and his eyes were chilling the group of women. Someone had raised her hand and bid six hundred, then it went to nine. But the auctioneer was stalled at one thousand. "Who'll give me one thousand? Do I hear one thousand?" And Callie just couldn't seem to twitch a finger in the direction of the auctioneer.

"One thousand. Do I hear…?"

Callie's arm was propelled into the air. By magic, she thought frantically, then realized it was Lindsay who had her by the elbow and was jerking her arm upward.

The auctioneer spotted her motion instantly and called out, "I have one thousand. Who'll give me twelve? Do I hear twelve hundred?"

Twelve never came, and Callie bought the mustached cop from Denver with the menacing look in his beautiful blue eyes.

"What a hoot," Lindsay whispered in her ear. "Now all you have to do is tame him." She turned to leave.

"Oh, God," Callie said desperately. "Don't leave me now, Lindsay."

But Lindsay kept right on going. "Just write the check and meet the man. How bad can it be?"

How bad...? A vision flew into Callie's befuddled mind.

Mase LeBow. Looking wickedly mean. Placing handcuffs on her wrists in a dark alley, dragging her into a patrol car. Locking her up. Throwing away the keys. And he was laughing, too, a deep male laugh utterly devoid of humor.

Someone was patting her on the back. Callie sucked in a big breath and focused. It was Rex Towbridge, the ranch director. "Great choice, Callie," he said, "but you bought him too cheap. Mase is a very special person."

Callie swallowed. "Is he...dangerous?"

Rex smiled warmly. "Mase? Heck, he's the nicest guy around. You got yourself a real bargain. Now, go and introduce yourself and have fun."

"Introduce myself?"

"Sure," Rex said. "You bought the man, Callie. He's yours, lock, stock and barrel."

Mase LeBow took the woman's proffered hand and shook it.

"Callie, Callie Thorne," she said, smiling, her

cheeks stained pink. "I—I guess I bought you, Mr. LeBow."

"Name's Mason," he said, looking down at her appraisingly. "People call me Mase."

"Mase," she said, and dropped her hand as if he'd burned her. "You're from, uh, from Denver?"

"That's right," he said, still eyeing her.

"You're a cop?"

"Homicide."

"Oh," she said. "My."

A heavy silence fell between them as they stood near the barbecue pit where Mase's son, Joey, was waiting in line for a piece of chicken.

Mase shifted his glance to Joey, checking on him, and then back to Callie Thorne. She looked as if she were about to die of embarrassment.

With the practiced eye of a cop, he assessed her quickly. She was about five foot seven in her boots, on the skinny side, with fine, blunt-cut dark gold hair that reached her shoulders beneath the cowgirl hat. She had great big round eyes, hazel and extremely expressive. Her cheekbones were high—still scarlet with what he took to be discomfort—and she had a wide, full-lipped mouth. Right now she was worrying her bottom lip with her teeth.

"We don't ever have murders in this neck of the woods," she said, and he had to fit his mind around her statement. He got it then. She was dwelling on his being a homicide detective.

"I don't imagine you do," he replied.

"No, never. Well, a few years back this man in Lightning Creek, he killed his wife. It was an accident, the sheriff concluded, but everyone thought he only made it look like an accident. You know.'' She shrugged and smiled feebly.

''Sure,'' Mase said.

There was something about her. He stared at the woman who'd bought a date with him and tried to get a handle on it. Something in her expression. Whimsy? It was as if her emotions were chasing themselves across her face like the shadows of wind-driven clouds racing across the prairie. Interesting, he thought. She wasn't beautiful, nor would he describe her as cute. The word *enchanting* flew into his head. He wanted to laugh. He could just see himself writing up a police report with her description on it. The guys would roll on the floor—''The suspect could be described as having an enchanting face.''

Joey was back, leaning on Mase's leg, hiding his head while he held on to the paper plate with the chicken. Mase wished he hadn't brought Joey along. All these people, strangers. It was hard on the boy. Ever since Mase had been widowed a year ago, Joey had been having a rough time of it. He was doing poorly at school, and often he was withdrawn, unreachable. Even the counselor the boy was seeing had been unable to crack his shell. Mase was worried. A lot more worried than he let on. He told himself he could handle his son's psychological condition, but the truth was, he was tortured with doubts as he lay in bed alone in the dark of the night.

He looked off into the distance, across the sage-dotted prairie to the hills beyond, and he frowned. There was an even more urgent problem right now. And Mase had made the six-hour drive from Denver to Lightning Creek mulling it over. He'd received a threatening phone call about Joey yesterday. If Mase testified in an upcoming, high-profile trial in Denver, Joey was going to pay for it. He could take a threat to his own safety, but to Joey's…?

Mase stood now in the brilliant sun, Joey clinging to him, Callie Thorne studiously looking at the toes of her dusty boots, and his frown darkened. Here he was, revisiting a place from his distant past, a special place where he'd discovered who he was and the direction his life would travel, and he was on a total bummer. He wouldn't have come at all after yesterday's call, except he had promised Rex Trowbridge, and Mase kept his promises.

Worse, he was being rude to this well-meaning lady who had just paid good money for a date.

He forced himself to concentrate on something she was saying.

"My folks' place is only a few miles away," Callie was telling him. "It's called the Someday Ranch. It's an equine therapy facility."

Mase cocked his dark head. "Equine therapy?"

She looked up and held his gaze. "Yes. Equine therapy is a highly successful form of treatment for the disabled, people with neuromuscular problems."

"Neuro…?"

"Nerve damage. Say, to the spine or a limb. People with cerebral palsy are great candidates for treatment. Or those with physical injuries or strokes. It can help a lot with emotional problems, too," she added, and he noticed her glance inadvertently flick to Joey for a second before she found Mase's eyes again. He would have said something defensive, but she was still talking. "I'm a therapist, a neuromuscular therapist specializing in the use of horses to bring about, well, small miracles with the guests at our ranch." One of those myriad emotions flitted across her face. Pride? Happiness?

"Small miracles," Mase said.

She nodded enthusiastically. "People respond to horses. It's a kind of magic," she said in earnest.

"Uh-huh," Mase replied. *Magic,* he thought. *Right.*

She was still chattering away, talking about the auction and how her friend Lindsay Duncan had talked her into participating. Mase wasn't paying a whole lot of attention. His thoughts were back on Joey and the upcoming murder trial at which he was scheduled to testify. He listened to Callie with only half an ear.

"I'm just so busy this summer," she was telling him. "So you're in luck."

"Luck," he repeated.

"Yes. I'm letting you off the hook. You don't have to go through with the date."

"Really," he said, distracted.

"The ranch is so isolated, anyway, and for you to have to get up here from Denver again would be such a hassle."

Isolated. Suddenly the wheels in his mind began to turn. He looked down at Joey, who was occupied with the chicken leg. *Isolated.* What if he could somehow get his son out of harm's way?

"Now," Callie said, smiling broadly, "isn't that magnanimous of me?"

"I'd like to see your ranch," Mase stated flatly.

"What?" Undisguised confusion clouded her features. She was staring at him, apparently baffled by his sudden desire to see her ranch.

Mase didn't reply but dragged his thoughts back to the auction, and he turned to listen to the ongoing cheers and whistles emanating from the showring. He knew most of the men being auctioned off, knew them from his years here at Lost Springs. From what he had gleaned, thanks to Rex and Sam Duncan and all the others, the vast majority of the men had turned their lives around. He sure had. He'd ended up here as a confused teen, having taken a stolen car for a joyride, and the juvenile judge had given his folks a choice: the Lost Springs Ranch or juvenile detention in a lockdown situation in western Colorado. His parents had opted for the ranch. It was the most important decision they'd ever made. An excellent choice. He'd spent his time here, finished high school and gone on to college in Denver. Then he'd decided on a career in law enforcement, gotten married, had Joey. If it hadn't been for this ranch, God knows where he might have ended up. Prison, most likely.

"Have you eaten?" a male voice asked. Mase turned to find that Rex and Lindsay had joined them. Rex patted Joey's head and grinned at Mase. "I see your boy found the barbecue. Have you tried the brownies, Joey?"

But Joey only hid his face again.

"He's shy," Lindsay said.

Mase gave them a shrug as if to agree. But *shy* had never been a word to describe Joey. What he'd been lately was withdrawn.

They talked some more about the auction and how far people had traveled to be here. Mase did his utmost to join in the conversation. It wasn't anyone's fault that he had gotten that threatening call, and he should try to be pleasant. It was hard, though. As they stood there talking, it occurred to him to wonder why Callie had picked him to bid on. He remembered that earlier she and Lindsay had actually studied him—as if he were a bull on the block—and Callie Thorne had been scowling.

Nevertheless, she had purchased a date with him, and he owed her his attention at the very least. He tried his best, but it wasn't easy with Joey clinging to his leg.

Eventually, Lindsay and Rex wandered back to the auction, and Mase turned his attention to Callie. "Well?" he said. "How about seeing your ranch?"

"You mean...*now?*" she replied.

"No time like the present," he answered, and he prayed she'd cave in.

For a long moment she only stared at him, then finally, mercifully, she nodded and said, "Okay, sure, why not?"

"Good," Mase said.

But she had to go and put a real damper on it by saying, "Maybe Joey could go for a ride on one of the horses."

He should have let it pass. But, damn, she was insinuating his son needed some sort of therapy. "I don't believe in that stuff, and I don't want my son on a horse," he said gruffly.

Callie paled. "I'm sorry. I didn't mean anything. Really."

But Mase was ticked off. "He's a little timid. Okay? The poor kid lost his mother last year, and he just needs some time to adjust." Mase realized he was clenching his jaw.

"I... Hey, I'm sorry, really," she said quickly. "I didn't know. I assumed you were divorced."

"Well, I'm not," he said tightly, and then he caught himself. What was he thinking? He might need this woman's help. The last thing he should be doing was alienating her.

"Listen," he said, and he ran his hand through his hair, "I'm sorry. I don't know why I went off like that."

"It's all right," Callie said. "It's perfectly understandable."

With that she walked away, mumbling something about needing a drink.

The auction ended an hour later, and Mase made it a point to find Callie in the crowd. He wasn't about to let her skip out on him.

"Oh, hi," she said when he and Joey walked up. "You still want to see the ranch, I guess."

"You bet," Mase said with false cheer.

He and Joey got in their car and followed her pickup truck. She'd said it wasn't far, a few miles. They traveled along a country road in the opposite direction from the town of Lightning Creek.

It was a glorious Wyoming afternoon in mid-June. Hot and bone-dry on the high prairie, the fields of tall native grasses blowing in the slight breeze, the sagebrush hills silvery in the late-afternoon sun. The potholed road followed a creek, winding toward the hills, crossing dry washes and deep cuts in the hard earth. To the west he could just make out the shape of the Rockies, dark pyramids against the blue sky. In Denver the foothills rose to the snowcapped peaks and the Continental Divide immediately to the west. But here, due north of Denver, the Rockies marched away well to the west, almost invisible except for the highest peaks.

It was a hard land. Hard to work on and hard to survive on. But the strong ones did. The Thornes, obviously, were among those. Tough folk. Ranchers.

The road straightened once they climbed the hills and descended the other side. A few miles, Callie had said. He guessed she meant on horseback, overland.

Mase glanced at the speedometer. Holy Toledo, he was doing seventy miles an hour and falling behind. This Callie was some kind of cowgirl.

He was thinking that when he heard the siren behind him. Despite being a cop, he felt his heart drop like lead to his stomach. He glanced into the rearview mirror and saw the flashing red-and-blue bar on the big Chevy Blazer—a typical county sheriff's cruiser.

He swore under his breath.

"Daddy," Joey said, "you aren't supposed to say that."

"I know, I know," Mase replied, and he stepped on the brakes and pulled onto the gravel shoulder.

The sheriff—his shiny ID badge read Reese Hatcher—sauntered up to Mase's window and began the litany. "License and registration, please." He had a real western twang to go along with a big belly, grizzled hair and a leathery face behind standard wire-rimmed sunglasses.

Mase shifted his weight and dug his wallet out of his back pocket. He smiled at Sheriff Reese Hatcher and flipped open the wallet, showing his very official police badge—equally as shiny as Hatcher's.

"This supposed to impress me?" the sheriff said.

"Well, no," Mase began, only vaguely aware that Callie's truck had stopped up ahead.

"Tell you what, sonny-boy," Hatcher continued, "this here Colorado badge don't mean squat up here."

"Well, I…" Mase started to say, but the sheriff held up a hand. Mase shut his mouth. Within minutes Hatcher had written up the ticket and was handing it to him through the open window—smiling the whole time.

Mase snatched the piece of paper. "Thanks," he mumbled, his jaw rock-hard. Then he looked up ahead toward the waiting pickup. "Why didn't you ticket *her?*" he said.

Slowly, the sheriff followed Mase's gaze. "Callie, you mean? Why, she wasn't speeding, was she?" he said, and he gave a big grin.

CHAPTER TWO

OOPS. CALLIE WATCHED Sheriff Hatcher climb back in his vehicle and drive away. Should she get out of her truck and apologize to Mase? Maybe she should call Reese Hatcher later and try to fix the ticket. Maybe… Oh boy, she'd done it now.

Not having the nerve to face Mase right then, she put her truck in gear and drove, sedately, carefully, agonizingly slowly, toward the Someday Ranch. She was relieved to see Mase follow. In the rearview mirror his face appeared set. God, he must be furious.

She turned onto the long rutted road that led to the ranch, stopped at the mailbox to pick up the day's mail, then drove through the triple-log uprights with the hand-carved sign across the top: Someday Ranch.

She pulled up alongside the house in her usual spot, turning off her engine, hearing the familiar diesel knock.

Mase parked next to her; he and Joey got out.

"Look," she said hastily, hopping down from the high truck seat, "I'm really sorry about that. I didn't realize we were going so fast."

"*I* was going too fast, but apparently *you* weren't," Mase said dryly.

"Sorry," she said, fumbling, feeling her cheeks heat up.

Jarod, Callie's assistant, strode by just then, leading

a dark brown horse, and Callie noticed that Joey shrank back and clung to his father.

"Hi, Callie," Jarod said, waving. "And who's this? Don't tell me, it's the guy you bought at the auction?"

"Hi, Jarod." She put a brave smile on her face. "This is him, all right. Mase LeBow, from Denver, and his son, Joey."

"Wow, Callie, looks like you got two for the price of one."

Jarod, with his wise-guy mouth, was a physical therapy student at the University of Wyoming who worked with her in the summers. She adored Jarod, who was blond and darling, but he had a way of patronizing her, even though he was ten years younger.

She introduced him to Mason, but that was only the beginning. The Someday Ranch was like a large, extended family: the patients—or guests, as they were called—and her father, Tom, who ran the ranch, and her mom, Liz, who took care of the books and all the patients' complicated health insurance forms. Then there was general aide and housemother Sylvia, a plump middle-aged woman with no children of her own, but a heart big enough to cherish every wounded soul who came to the ranch. The cook was Francine, a tiny skinny lady with red hair, whose gruff manner hid her warmth. The animals were also a big part of the ranch. There were the horses, specially chosen and trained for their job; two oversize mutts, Beavis and Butt-Head, who loved everyone indiscriminately; and assorted cats, who were supposed to keep the barn vermin-free, but who were fed by Francine and mostly lay around and slept.

Beavis and Butt-Head came bounding over now. "Down!" Callie yelled, preparing for the onslaught, but they both went straight to Mase, looked up at him with adoration and wagged their lethal tails. Beavis gave Joey a wet swipe with his pink tongue as an aside.

Joey looked as if he were going to cry.

"Beavis kissed you," Callie said, smiling at Joey. "He must really like you, because usually he just jumps on people."

Joey's small face turned up to her. "It felt funny."

"That's a dog kiss. You'll get used to it," she said, and she met Mase's gaze over his son's head. She winked at him, and saw a faint smile tug at the corner of his mouth. His hand rested protectively on Joey's head.

Jarod was taking the horse to the barn, a weathered red building that sat across the broad driveway, its double doors gaping open.

"That's where this horse Kahlua gets her dinner," Callie was telling Joey. "She's worked hard today. And that's the indoor ring." She pointed to the big enclosure connected to the barn. "We ride in there when it's not nice out. And those two buildings are where the guests stay, the bunkhouses, we call them."

Joey was listening to her, which was good. He appeared interested, not so frightened at the moment. Beavis gave him another wet lick, but this time Joey didn't shrink away.

"Would you like to pet Kahlua?" Callie asked him. Then to Mase she added, "If you don't mind. I've got to check in with Jarod, anyway. Then we'll go into the house and you can meet everyone else. It's almost time for dinner."

"I don't want to inconvenience you," Mase began.

"Come on, then," she replied, heading toward the barn.

Callie breathed in the wonderful rich aroma of the barn with pleasure, as she always did. Stalls lined the wide center aisle, and a dozen horses of every size and shape were peacefully munching their evening grain. Later they'd be turned out to pasture for the night, where they'd graze in the rich, irrigated fields.

Jarod was finishing brushing Kahlua, ready to put her in a stall with her bucket of grain.

"How'd it go today?" Callie asked him.

"Fine."

"How was Hal?"

"Great. He felt his knees, and his balance was much better. He hardly needs any help getting on now. He's a strong kid."

"*Kid,*" Callie snorted. "He's your age."

Jarod ignored her. "So, Mr. LeBow," he said, "do you ride horses?"

Mase gave a short laugh. "I've been on a few, but I just don't have the right touch."

"You had to ride when you were at Lost Springs, didn't you?" Callie asked, surprised.

"Oh, yeah, I did, but after a while the instructor let me run laps instead."

"What a shame," Callie said, her head cocked, studying him. "You look so...so competent, too."

Mase shrugged. "I am also a competent driver, despite my recent run-in with the law."

"The what?" Jarod asked.

So Callie had to tell the story. Embarrassed, swearing silently she'd never drive over fifty-five again, she told Jarod, who laughed like an idiot.

It was then that she noticed Joey's severe discomfort. He cringed behind Mase, obviously keeping his father between him and the horse, and his face was white. He was scared to death of the big brown mare who stood there, idly swishing her tail at flies, waiting for her dinner. Poor Joey, and Callie hadn't even noticed.

Instantly she kneeled down next to the boy. "Joey," she said, "hey, Joey, this is Kahlua. She's a female, a mare. She's big, isn't she? But she has to be big and strong so people can ride on her back."

No response.

"Maybe we better go," Mase began to say, but Callie shook her head.

"Would you like to hear the story of how Kahlua came to the ranch, Joey? She's a very special mare. Well, she was real sick, almost starving to death. You could feel every one of her ribs. No one wanted her, and if one of my friends hadn't called me and told me about her, well, I don't know what would have happened to her." But Callie did know. Kahlua would have been sold for a few hundred dollars, loaded on a truck and taken to the meat packers. Not that she'd tell Joey that.

The boy's eyes cut toward the horse. He was listening. Good.

"So I hitched up the horse trailer and went and picked her up, and we took care of her and she got better. Now she's one of our best therapy horses, and she helps people who have problems. She especially likes boys like you."

Joey's eyes switched from Callie's face up to the tall brown horse then back again. "She was sick?" he asked.

Callie nodded. "She could hardly walk."

"But she's better now." It wasn't a question.

"All better. Uh-huh."

Joey studied the mare. His face had lost the pinched look.

"You want your dad to lift you up so you can see her?" Callie asked.

The boy nodded. Mase hoisted Joey up, so that he was face-to-face with the mare. She reached her head out toward him, and he drew back.

"She thinks you have her dinner," Callie said. "She knows it's mealtime. Would you like to give her a horse cookie?"

Joey shook his head.

"Okay, I will, then." Callie went to a bin in the tack room and came back with a handful of nuggets of compressed sweet hay and held one out to the mare in the palm of her hand. Kahlua fluttered her nostrils, whickered deep in her chest and deftly lipped the cookie from Callie's hand.

"See? She's hungry," Callie said.

"Does she like the cookies?" Joey asked.

"She loves them." Callie held out another, and Kahlua whisked it away. "You sure you don't want to try?"

"Well…"

"Hold your hand flat, like this. Her whiskers tickle. You can feel her breath. See how her lip moves. Did you know a horse's lip is almost like an elephant's trunk? It is, really. She can move it every whichaway."

Callie held her hand under Joey's small grubby one, laid a cookie on his palm and reached out toward the mare, who snatched the treat. Joey drew his hand back with a gasp.

"It tickled, didn't it?" Callie asked.

"Uh-huh."

Callie stroked Kahlua's nose. "Do you want to pet her, Joey? She likes that."

Tentatively, he put his hand out. The mare flicked her ears, looking for another cookie, and Joey touched her velvety nose, first with one finger, then with his hand. As Callie watched, a smile formed on his face, and he lost the tension that had held his small body in its grip.

"Daddy, she's warm," Joey said.

"Sure she is," Mase replied in a tone Callie hadn't heard from him before.

She watched the little boy and his father, and Joey's need—*their* need—cried out to her. Then she wondered if fate had staged the whole bachelor auction simply to get the LeBow men here, right now. Maybe they both needed a little of the ranch's magic.

The sun was low in the sky when they left Kahlua contentedly munching her grain.

"Everyone's probably already gathering for dinner," Callie explained. "You'll have to meet the whole crew."

"Maybe Joey and I should take off now," Mase said. "It was nice of you to show us your place and let Joey pet the horse, but I think—"

"Oh, no, you don't. You're here, and you'll have to satisfy their curiosity. They've probably all been spying on you from the house."

Mase shot a swift glance toward the ranch house, as if he expected mayhem to erupt from its doors and windows. But it sat serenely in the setting sun, surrounded by cottonwoods, a turreted yellow Victorian farmhouse trimmed with white gingerbread, with a deep porch and a few additions tacked on in unlikely places.

"You're joking," he said.

"Nope."

They walked across the driveway and along the flower-lined sidewalk, up the stairs and into the shadow of the porch. As Callie reached out to open the door, one of her visions popped into her head.

Her folks and the staff and guests were all waiting for dinner, laughing and chatting, when Callie and Mase and Joey entered. Instant and total silence fell. All heads turned toward them as if on cue, and everyone stared. There they stood, the object of all that attention. Callie looked down and her clothes were melting away. In a panic, she looked at Mase, and his clothes were melting, too, and everybody was pointing and whispering.

The reality wasn't quite like that, but not far off.

Her tall, lanky father, Tom, approached them right away and was introduced, then her mom, Liz, and Sylvia. Jarod nodded hello, and Callie introduced the four adult guests, Hal, Marianne, James and Linda, and the two children, Rebecca and Peter. Francine popped out of the kitchen, drying her hands on her apron to look him up and down as if measuring him for a pot on her stove.

Joey hid his face, hanging on to Mase's leg. Frankly, Callie didn't blame him.

"I really don't want to impose…" Mase began, but was immediately interrupted.

"What's one or two more mouths?" Francine said. "The food's not fancy, but it's good."

"No, really, Joey and I have to get back."

"Got a date?" Sylvia asked pointedly.

"Well, no, but…"

"You'll stay then, good," Liz said, smiling. "Joey looks really hungry."

"Like Kahlua," Joey said in a tiny voice.

"You bet, just like Kahlua," Liz agreed.

"If you don't mind, it would be great," Mase said, giving in.

Dinner was a noisy affair, served family-style around a big oak table. Tonight it was beef stew, a fresh green salad, sourdough rolls and cherry pie for dessert.

Tom had placed Mase between himself and Callie. She couldn't help but notice how well her father got along with Mase. And how pleasant Mase appeared when he spoke to Tom.

"So, you're a homicide detective," Tom was saying. "What an interesting job."

"Oh, it's interesting, all right," Mase said flatly.

"It must be tough."

"It can be, yeah."

Callie tried to picture Mase at his job, doing the things she saw cops do on TV and in the movies. Yes, she could imagine him being hard and unforgiving, interviewing suspects, unrelenting in his pursuit of criminals. Sure, and she bet that's why he hardly smiled. He would see evil day in and day out in his job. He must have a hard time believing good of anyone. That must have been why he'd looked so menacing on the auction block. Sure. That explained it.

She sneaked a sidelong glance at him. His profile was handsome, a well-shaped nose, sensual lips, a lock of dark hair falling across his forehead, the neat mustache. He was listening intently to Tom, asking something once in a while.

At the other end of the table, Joey sat with twelve-year-old Peter, who chatted incessantly, and little Rebecca was on Joey's other side, but she ate silently, her eyes downcast. Callie wasn't sure who needed more love and attention, Joey or Rebecca.

Jarod was asking Mase something; Callie tuned in to the conversation. "Do you carry a gun?"

"Well, not now," Mase said, "but at work I do."

"Have you ever been shot at?" Jarod wanted to know.

Mase shrugged. "Once. He missed. Mostly my work is investigatory. It's actually quite boring, following leads, lining up witnesses."

"Boring," Jarod said, disbelieving.

"It's not like in the movies," Mase replied, "believe me."

Callie noticed that he had a healthy appetite and seemed to enjoy Francine's food. She wondered what he cooked at home, and how he managed working and taking care of his son. She wondered if he went out much, had a steady girlfriend, dated casually. Or did he stay home at night like she did? Single, thirty-something, and isolated on a ranch. Busy every waking moment, dedicated to her work, rarely meeting eligible men—that was Callie in a nutshell. Was it the same for Mase?

Of course not. For one thing, Mase had been married and he had a child. Callie was a stranger to those experiences, and she suddenly envied him. What had his wife been like? How much did he miss her?

So many questions.

"You have a great place here," Mase was saying to Tom. "Peaceful."

"Well, it can get hectic, but it's a pretty darn good life." Tom looked at him. "You're welcome to stay the night, check the place out. Go for a horseback ride tomorrow.''

"Thanks, but I really do have to get back to Denver tomorrow. I appreciate the invitation. Maybe some other time.''

He had a nice voice, Callie decided. Deep and smooth. She bet it could turn into steel when he questioned criminals, though. Oh, yes.

"Good choice, Callie,'' Sylvia called from across the table. "Your taste is improving.''

"Oh, go bid for your own guy,'' Callie shot back, and Sylvia laughed.

Callie knew what the housemother meant, though. Callie had had bad luck with men, seeming to go only for losers, the needy ones who invariably let her down. The last guy had been a rodeo circuit rider who'd left Callie for a Boston debutante.

That had been six months ago. Dating was difficult living out here on the ranch. Sometimes Callie felt her biological clock ticking away, but mostly she didn't think about it—she was too occupied with dispensing her own personal brand of joy and hope.

"Five hundred acres,'' Tom said, replying to a question of Mase's. "Backed by Forest Service land. Heck, I don't use all of it. Got some acreage in hay, some in oats. Good water rights. It suits us fine.''

Her parents weren't at all sure ranch life suited Callie, though. They often asked her if she wouldn't be better off in a city, or a town, at least. They'd offered to help her set up a therapy practice in Casper or Laramie or anywhere else she'd like to consider. They were concerned about her social life—or lack thereof—but they didn't understand how necessary it was to stay here, that it was the ranch setting that gave a special magic to her work.

Her mother and Sylvia told Callie that staying on the ranch and purposely picking losers was her way of avoiding a commitment, a disease among singles these days. They pestered her with this theory all the time, pecking away at her like hens. They meant well, she knew, but she'd learned to ignore them.

Mase was speaking again, and Callie tuned back in. She wished he'd say something personal, something that would help her understand him better, but he was only talking about crime in the city.

"Yeah, the young kids are vulnerable to that. And the gangs have been filtering in from California for a few years now. Drive-by shootings, the whole thing."

"Denver's a big city," Tom said.

"And growing like crazy. Traffic, crime. It's hard for me to believe how it's changed."

"You can't turn back the clock," Tom said. "Things change."

"True enough." Mase looked down at his empty plate. "That pie was great. I haven't eaten this much in months."

"Glad you enjoyed it," Tom said.

Well, Mase and her father were certainly hitting it off. He hadn't said a word to her, though. What was he doing here, anyway? Why had he stayed for dinner? She'd told him he didn't have to fulfill the date obligation.

Questions and more questions.

She'd like to ask him outright, but that would be rude. And what did she care, anyway? After tonight, she'd probably never see him again.

When dinner was over, everyone helped with the

cleanup. Callie and her parents accompanied Mase and Joey out to the car.

"I've got to get back to the motel and get Joey to bed," Mase said. "Thanks so much for the delicious meal. Tell Francine how much I enjoyed it." He turned to Callie. "Thanks for bringing me to your home. I've enjoyed meeting everyone."

She waved a hand airily. "Oh, no problem. You got off easy. If you'd stuck around, they'd have put you to work."

"There are worse things to work at," he said. "Joey, tell everyone thanks."

"Thank you," the little boy whispered. Then he added, "Daddy, can we come back?"

For the first time Mase seemed flustered. "Well, I don't know. We'll see. It depends."

"Any time," Liz offered warmly.

Callie kneeled down in front of Joey. "I hope you can come back and visit. Kahlua will be waiting for you." Then she gave Joey a hug.

"Look," Mase said to her, "I'd appreciate it if you don't give him unrealistic expectations."

"Those are the best kind," Callie replied, undaunted.

He frowned. "Come on, Joey."

Her folks went inside, but Callie stood on the porch in the darkness and watched Mase and his son climb into their car, start it up and back out. The car's headlights cut a silver swath across fields and barn and house as Mase headed down the driveway.

Phew, Callie thought, immensely glad the day was over. But she'd survived it. You bet she had. It had been a heck of a way to spend a thousand dollars, too, and a heck of a short date. The question was, had she gotten her money's worth?

"Nah," she muttered, and she strode on back inside.

CHAPTER THREE

CALLIE GOT OUT OF BED late the next morning and decided it was the excitement of the auction that had worn her out.

She showered and brushed her hair, and despite herself she couldn't stop wondering about Mase. She could see him in her mind's eye, those blue eyes, the sensual curve of his mouth under his mustache just before he'd smiled at something her father had said. And the hard line of those same lips. He seemed to have reserved that for her alone. Did he resent the auction? Perhaps he'd felt belittled by her having bid for him. She couldn't make him out at all. On the other hand, he was gone now, out of her life. And that was just fine with her.

It was a busy day. But then every day was busy, especially in the summer months, when everyone wanted to be outdoors. The Someday Ranch had a big indoor ring that was heated, but the guests responded so much better to the therapy sessions when they were held outside.

Wyoming in the winter could be the cruelest place. Unbearable winds blew down out of the Rockies for months on end, lowering already freezing temperatures by another twenty degrees or so.

But summer was heaven. Incredibly clear blue skies and low humidity. It was warm, but never too hot, not when the air was so dry. The guests, especially those from the humid east, perked up for any challenge.

Before heading out to begin Hal's therapy session, Callie had a bowl of cereal in the kitchen with Francine and her mother. She just knew someone was going to bring up the subject of Mase LeBow. It wasn't in this crew to let a sleeping dog lie.

Her mom was the culprit this morning. "Such a nice man, Callie," Liz said from across the big wooden worktable.

"Who?" Callie asked innocently.

"Mase," Francine put in. "If you don't want him, I'll be happy to make that date."

"I think the date's already over," Callie said. "He visited the ranch, we had dinner and all." She shrugged.

Liz cocked her head. "You mean that was *it?* You paid all that money for a couple of hours?"

Callie looked up from her bowl. "I told him he didn't have to go through with the thing, the silly date. I mean, the guy's all the way down in Denver and I'm up here. What would be the point?"

"A date," Francine said. "The whole point is a date with a handsome man. You paid for it. Now, if he was obnoxious or something, sure, I'd have let him off the hook, too. But Mase…"

"Can we drop it, please?" Callie asked, cutting in. "I don't think we particularly hit it off. The vibes just didn't flow. Okay?"

Francine made a disapproving noise, and Liz only stared pensively at her daughter.

HAL HAD BEEN wheelchair-bound since a college football accident eighteen months ago left him with a bruised spinal cord. He was already waiting by the ring, where he would ride Milky Way today. His was the first of the therapy sessions Callie would give that day. Jarod had six scheduled. Between the three morning sessions and then lunch, some ranch work and three more afternoon therapy sessions, her day was booked.

"Morning, Hal," Callie said as she untied Milky Way from the fence. "You look chipper."

"I'm okay, I guess," Hal said.

He'd been a tough nut to crack when he had arrived a month ago. He had seemed sullen and withdrawn, carrying the biggest weight on his shoulders that Callie had ever seen. It had taken a full week to get Hal onto a horse's back, and he had only done it because his new friend Marianne, another patient, had called him a wimp for not giving the therapy a shot.

After his very first ride Callie had seen improvement in him. For the first time since his spinal injury, Hal had legs again. Okay, so they weren't his, but he was afforded the simple pleasure of freedom of movement. Even Marianne saw the improvement in him. Marianne was a wonderful patient, never down, always optimistic and a hard worker, to boot. She was recovering from a head injury after a car accident. To tell the truth, Callie depended on her good cheer, especially with Hal. The benefits of the therapy depended as much on encouragement, trust and enthusiasm as they did on physical training. The kids got kisses and hugs, the adults got subtler encouragement, but it was all directed at positive reinforcement, a can-do attitude. And it worked. Once Hal was mounted, Jarod led the brown-and-white-spotted Milky Way. Callie walked on one side, her dad on the other, supporting Hal. His balance was so much better that they were hardly needed. Callie talked him through the routine, directing him to move his arms above his head, bend one way, then the other. Much of the physical benefit came simply from sitting on the horse, feeling the animal's gait precisely reproduce the movement of the human pelvis when walking.

Hal had been told he might very well regain the use of his legs, but the doctors couldn't be sure; sometimes the trauma to the spinal cord healed completely, sometimes partially. Patience and time had been their advice. But Hal had been impatient and getting depressed, so his parents found the Someday Ranch, and they were everlastingly thankful.

Hal had begun asking lately if he could go on a trail ride. Not yet, Callie had told him. Not until he could get on a horse unassisted. So he worked at it, and Marianne encouraged him.

There was something developing between the two of them—everyone at the ranch had noticed—and it was a bond that was strengthening every day. Even Hal's parents, who'd visited a week ago from Kansas City, had been aware of it. And they'd been thrilled.

Callie finished the session with Hal by critiquing his performance. He was used to hard-driving football coaches, so she saved her hugs and kisses for other patients and gave him what he wanted. "All right, that was a good recovery when Milky Way stopped short. I'd like you to try to put more weight in the stirrups. I know, I know, you can't feel your feet, but imagine it. Imagining, Hal, is very important. You used to imagine how to throw the football, how you'd make a certain play, right?"

"Yeah."

"Same thing here. It's coming back, all those little

muscles, all the nerves. They need training, like a million little athletes.''

''Okay, coach.''

Callie grinned and gave Hal a not-so-light punch in the biceps. ''Tomorrow, right?''

Peter came bounding over to the ring, running into the center.

''Slow down there, cowboy,'' Callie said to the twelve-year-old, who had attention deficit disorder. ''You know the horses don't like sudden movements around them.''

Peter, who would do anything to please the animals, came to an abrupt halt. ''Sorry. I forgot.''

Callie smiled. ''It's okay. Did you have your session with Jarod yet?''

''After lunch,'' Peter said, fidgeting while Callie unsaddled Milky Way.

Peter was climbing the rails to the ring, and Callie watched him for a moment. So much energy.

She smiled, shaking her head, and was turning back to the horse when she saw a look, a peculiar blank expression on Peter's face.

''Peter,'' she said softly, ''are you okay?''

He seemed to come back into himself and focused on her. ''You know that man who was here yesterday? With Joey?''

''Yes,'' Callie said, lifting the heavy saddle. ''That was Joey's dad.''

''That man's in trouble.''

Callie stopped in her tracks. Since Peter's arrival at the ranch a month ago, everyone had become aware of the special gift he possessed: he was clairvoyant. At first, when he was learning to focus and concentrate, no one had believed Callie about his ability to ''see'' things. But then Peter started finding misplaced items around the guest bunkhouse and even in the main house. A pocketknife. A pair of reading glasses. And once, when his parents came for an unannounced visit from Casper, Peter had known they were coming.

He had said, "Mommy and Daddy are in the car getting gas in Lightning Creek. They'll be here for lunch."

Sure enough, just as everyone was gathering in the main house, Peter's parents drove up.

Callie studied the boy now. "Why do you think Mr. LeBow is in trouble?"

Peter looked her squarely in the eye. "'Cause he is. Well, Joey is."

Then Callie thought she understood. Since the death of Joey's mother, the child had become despondent. Yes. That was trouble of a sort. And it couldn't be easy on Mase, either.

Callie smiled at Peter and picked the saddle up, accepting his statement as another one of his uncanny insights.

For the many success stories at the Someday Ranch, there were always a few failures. Very few. But enough to unsettle everyone. Rebecca Brown, who had recently had her sixth birthday, was not responding to the therapy as well as the staff had hoped.

Rebecca was autistic and hadn't spoken a word in over a year, not since she had witnessed her baby brother take a fall. Her brother recovered fully from the injuries, but the trauma of the experience had sent Rebecca into a silent place.

Her parents had tried everything, but nothing had worked. So far. In desperation they'd brought her to the Someday Ranch. She'd been here for two months, and Callie was awfully afraid her parents were going to take her home if she didn't show at least a little improvement soon.

Callie worked very hard with the child until lunchtime, and Rebecca showed the usual bonding with the horse she was riding. But she was oblivious to all but the movement of the horse's smooth, firm back beneath her. Callie so desperately wanted Rebecca to speak again. She even dreamed about her at night, saw her speaking to Kahlua, running and laughing with Beavis and Butt-Head at her heels. It wasn't going to happen today. Tomorrow, though, Callie mused, Rebecca would speak tomorrow. At lunch she told everyone that, and they all agreed. Sure, Rebecca would respond any day now. But no one at the ranch believed as wholeheartedly as Callie did. They all thought she was a bit of a dreamer.

The call from Mase came on Wednesday after dinner. Callie could not have been more surprised. She took the cordless phone from Sylvia and found a private spot, sitting on the top step of the staircase in the main house.

"Hello?" she said.

"Callie?"

"Yes, this is Callie. Is that you, Mase?" She couldn't believe it. What on earth had compelled him to call? Had he left something here?

"Yeah," he was saying, "it's me. I just wanted to touch base about our date. I didn't mean to go rushing off the other evening without setting the time and place."

"Our...date?" she said stupidly.

"Sure. You didn't think I'd fink out on it, did you?"

"Well, no, but like I told you, it's not necessary to go through with it. You're busy. I'm maxed." She caught her lower lip with her teeth, then released it. "It's very nice of you to call, though."

"I insist," he said. "And I was hoping we could do it right at your ranch."

"Do…the date?"

"Yes, Callie, the date. The only trouble is my parents won't be able to watch Joey next weekend, so I'll have to bring him along. Is that all right?"

Next weekend?

"Callie? You still there?"

"I, ah, well, of course Joey can come. I mean, if you come, that is. But you don't have to. Really."

"I insist," he said. "I'll drive up a week from this Friday, as soon as I can get off work. Is that okay?"

"Of course," Callie said, "a week from Friday. I'll have Francine hold dinner."

"Thanks," he said. "See you then."

"Oh, sure," she said, "I'm looking forward to it."

But when she was off the phone, she had a sudden image of a huge yellow bulldozer, and its treads had just run over her.

LUNCH IN TOWN with Lindsay was Callie's idea. She called Lindsay on Saturday morning and said she was dying to hear all about the end results of the auction and, hey, why not meet in Lightning Creek at the Roadkill Grill around noon?

"It's a date," Lindsay said.

But when Callie was driving toward town, she realized she hadn't been entirely honest. Yes, she wanted to hear about the auction, but there was another subject bedeviling her: Mase LeBow.

She thought a lot about that as she drove—keeping her speed under control this time—along the Shoshone Highway. Why was she so darn curious about the man?

She took Poplar Road into Lightning Creek, stopped for gas at Chuck's Exxon station, then headed down Main Street. The street curved around the town landmark, the statue of a cowboy on a bucking bronco, arm thrown up in the air, then continued on. She found a parking spot in front of Twyla's Tease 'n' Tweeze beauty salon. The sign out front was emblazoned with Twyla's signature logo, a pair of ruby slippers just like those worn by Dorothy in *The Wizard of Oz*. Callie got out of the truck and headed for the grill. She had dressed for the occasion. Usually she never got out of her jeans and Stetson. Today, though, she had put on a khaki miniskirt, a sleeveless yellow-flowered cotton top and high-heeled sandals. The sandals were a pain in the butt to drive with, but they were terribly stylish, and Callie loved the clip-clop sound they made on the sidewalk.

Lindsay was already seated at a window booth and waved Callie over. "What a treat," Lindsay said. "When's the last time we had lunch together in town?"

Callie ordered an iced tea and shook her head. "Can't remember. Ages, I guess. So tell me all about the auction. Did you make a bundle for the boys?"

They spent an hour talking about the men, and who had bought whom and for how much.

"What about you?" Callie asked. "You made me buy someone, but you…"

"Oh, you know, I bid on Rex."

"No fair, Lindsay, you already know him."

"That was the point," Lindsay said defensively. "It let us both off the hook."

Callie rolled her eyes. "Unfair, unfair. How come you two got off easy?"

"Because, Thorne, we organized the whole she-bang." Then Lindsay changed the subject. "So," she said, "I got all the info for you after you called."

"Huh?" Callie looked up from her apple pie à la mode.

"You called me about lunch 'cause you wanted to pump me about Mase."

"I most certainly did not."

Lindsay shrugged. "Anyway, I talked to Rex and I've got the whole scoop. Of course, if you aren't interested—" Lindsay glanced at her wristwatch "—I do have to get back to Lost Springs."

Callie sighed. "Tell me."

"Only if you admit that's why you really called."

"God, I hate you. Okay, yes, it's a part of why I called. Satisfied?"

"Thoroughly." Lindsay grinned like the Cheshire cat, then her expression softened. "Okay, here goes. Mase originally came to the ranch after he stole a car and proceeded to drive it into Cherry Creek in Denver."

"Right into the creek?"

"Rex reminded me of it. I think it was a Mercedes. I guess the owner of the car was a lawyer, and he knew the juvenile judge and wanted the book thrown at Mase."

"But he ended up here."

Lindsay nodded. "I remember he was a real hellion at first, but then settled in okay. By the time he left he was actually ready for college. I don't know how he got into law enforcement, but I do know he was married for some time."

"I learned that the hard way," Callie said. "I mean, that he wasn't divorced, but that his wife died. Last year, I think."

"Car accident," Lindsay told her.

Car accident, Callie thought. Oh, Lordy, the speeding ticket Mase got because of her...

"Anyway," Lindsay was saying, "he's involved in this big murder case in Denver. Mase is the star witness. Have you ever heard the name Richard Metcalf?"

Callie frowned, thinking. The name was ringing a bell, but she couldn't remember who he was.

"Metcalf is the guy who's been bidding to build that new super sports complex in Denver."

"Oh, right," Callie said. "Really rich guy."

"That's him. Anyway, this city councilman was murdered. And I guess Mase can tie Richard Metcalf to the murder."

"Wow," Callie breathed.

"Rex and Sam have been following it, and then said it has something to do with Metcalf trying to bribe the city councilman, but the man wouldn't go along, so, allegedly, Metcalf hired someone to snuff him."

Callie sat back in her seat. "That's...big. I mean, that Mase is involved and all. And he actually *saw* the murder?"

"I don't think he saw it. Rex said he was at the scene within minutes and bumped right into the hitman. He can ID the man, and the man's connected to Metcalf."

Callie was shaking her head. "And Mase LeBow wants to go out with me? Come on."

"Why not?"

"It's ridiculous. Why, he must be a local hero. Every

woman in Denver has to be hot for him, Lindsay. Why would he waste his time with me? And at the Someday Ranch? It's absurd.''

Lindsay frowned. ''Did it ever occur to you that maybe he was attracted?''

''Not in a million years,'' Callie said staunchly.

She thought about everything Lindsay had told her all afternoon. At dinner she was still thinking about it. She took Peter and Rebecca for a ride that evening and could barely concentrate on anything else except Mase and the murder trial. That night she stood in front of the mirror in her pajamas and took a long, hard look at herself. Skinny legs, and not very shapely at that. She turned sideways and pulled her pajama top tight, studying her flat chest and sighing. ''Ugh,'' she said.

Her hair. She had the most godawful baby-fine hair. If Twyla didn't blunt cut it at least once a month it was hopeless.

Okay. Her face wasn't too bad. At least she wasn't a complete dog. But special enough to attract Mase? No way.

He'd called her, though. She'd sat on the staircase and talked to him on the phone, and he'd insisted on keeping the date. Why?

For Joey? But no. Mase was in complete denial about his son's problems, and the last thing on his mind was therapy for Joey.

Could Mase really have been attracted to her? Lindsay thought so. But what did Lindsay know, anyway?

So if Mase wasn't making the long trip to Wyoming again to see her or to help his boy, why, then, was he doing this?

She climbed into bed, pulled the sheet up under her chin and stewed. *Mase LeBow, what are you really after?*

CHAPTER FOUR

SINCE MASE HAD RETURNED from the auction over a week ago, he'd barely let Joey out of his sight. It was especially hard now that school was out. He was afraid to send Joey to day care or summer camp because of the threat, so he was depending on his parents to help out.

It was rough. He had to work, and a homicide detective worked odd hours. If it hadn't been for his folks, Mase didn't know what he would have done.

On Tuesday morning he dropped Joey off at his parents' house in the Denver suburb of Castle Pines. Mase's mom didn't know about the threat to Joey, though Mase had told his dad the whole truth. Still, Brenda LeBow knew something was up. After all, Mase was her son, and he'd never been able to hide things from her. To her credit, she didn't ask. On that Tuesday morning, all she said was that they'd take good care of Joey and for Mase not to worry.

"Thanks, Mom," Mase said, and he kissed her cheek. Then he knelt down and tousled Joey's dark hair. "You be good for Grandma and Grandpa, hear?"

Joey nodded sullenly and looked as if he were about to cry. God, how Mase hated leaving him. Even with his own folks. Joey simply wasn't responding to anyone but Mase.

Brenda picked her grandson up and kissed him. "I

baked cinnamon rolls,'' she said. ''Come on, let's go have one before Grandpa eats them all.''

That, at least, got Joey's attention, and he followed his grandmother inside. Mase gave them both a wave and took off for Denver, guilt weighing heavily on his shoulders. Soon, though, Joey would be on the ranch and out of harm's way. The trial was still weeks off and Mase didn't know how he was going to talk the Thornes into keeping his son there. Of course, he would pay for Joey to stay, but the whole thing seemed so devious. He couldn't tell them the truth, though. The only people he had told were his dad and his boss. Lately, Mase really didn't know who else he could trust. Maybe his partner, Luke. Luke was okay. But he didn't dare confide in the Thornes.

What could he say to them, anyway? How could he tell the complicated story? He tried to frame it in his mind.

He saw himself sitting in their cozy living room casual-like, and he'd say, ''Well, Mr. and Mrs. Thorne—Tom and Liz—and you, too, Callie, there's this wealthy guy named Richard Metcalf who is threatening my son....'' He'd go on to tell them about Metcalf's attempt to bribe a Denver city councilman named Edwards. When Edwards threatened to make the bribery attempt public, Metcalf must have panicked, and Edwards was found murdered. Mase was pretty sure the killer was a hired hitman named Hank Berry.

Mase imagined the looks of horror on the faces of the three Thornes. Bribery, a killer, a murder. But he would already have gone too far.

Tom Thorne would say, ''Lord Almighty, and you're involved in this?''

''Well, not on purpose, sir,'' he'd say, but he'd still

have to tell them the whole ugly story. "You see, I was on duty when the councilman heard a noise and got scared one night and called 911. I was close to his building, and I got to the scene so quickly that I ran right into Berry—better known as the Hitman—outside Edwards's building. I didn't know at the time, of course, that I had just come face-to-face with a man who'd committed murder minutes ago. It was just pure luck that when I did bump into him, I got a good look at him. At this point," he'd say, "the district attorney got a legal wiretap put on Metcalf's phone. With a couple of recorded conversations between Metcalf and Berry, and me as the pivotal witness, we had Metcalf dead to rights. Still do."

"So, what's the problem?" Liz would ask.

"Well," Mase would say, at this point unable to meet Callie's eyes, "we still can't find Hank Berry. There are nationwide APBs out on him, but he's as slippery as an eel. And, well, there's another little hitch...."

"Yes?" Callie would ask, getting suspicious.

"Er," Mase would mumble, "there's uh, there's been a threat to Joey's life and, well, I just thought that he'd be safe here, you know, at the Someday Ranch, and that way I'll be safe to testify. Jeez, I hope you don't think I'm using you...."

"Golly, no," they'd all say at once.

Right, Mase thought.

What a mess.

As he drove north on I-25 toward police headquarters, Mase kept thinking about the Hitman. He'd bet a year's salary it was Berry who'd made the threatening call about Joey. Metcalf wouldn't have the nerve, he thought as he parked in the lot across from headquarters.

He entered the huge building and went through security, then took the elevator up to Homicide. The place was buzzing. The only time it was quiet in the big department was at night, and even then there were a couple of guys coming and going, answering calls. Mase used to like the night shift. But now, well, he needed to be home for Joey.

He checked in with Captain Al Coleman, his immediate superior, and got the assignments for the day. Another drive-by shooting in north Denver. Gang related. "Swell," Mase said under his breath.

"Any more calls? Threats?" Coleman asked, looking up.

Mase shook his head. "So far just the one."

"It's enough. I'd like to get you and your boy out of here till the trial."

"I told you about the plans for Joey," Mase began. "The ranch in Wyoming."

"I know. And I like it. But you're probably a target, too."

"The Hitman's not gonna kill a cop."

"You seem pretty sure of that," Coleman said flatly. "Remember, he's not above threatening a cop's kid."

Al had a point, Mase knew. Still, he wasn't going to tuck tail and run. He shrugged and strode to the captain's door. "I've got Joey covered," he said, "and I can damn well handle myself."

"I hope you're right," Coleman said pointedly.

Mase said hi to a few of his fellow detectives, then checked his mail slot. The usual stuff. There was one unusual piece, however, and he stood eyeing the little white envelope curiously. An invitation? He started to-

ward his partner's desk, opening the envelope, when
he noticed a scent rising from the paper. Automatically,
Mase put it to his nose. Vanilla?

"Hey, Luke," he said in greeting when he reached
his partner's desk. "Be with you in a sec."

"We got a shooting to investigate in north Denver,"
Luke said.

"Yeah, yeah, I know," Mase replied, distracted as
he unfolded the vanilla-scented card and began to read.

Dear Mase,
I hope this reaches you, as I don't have your home
address. I only wanted to drop you a note and
apologize if I was rude the other night on the
phone. Of course you and Joey are both very welcome at the ranch, and I still hope to see you
Friday evening. Maybe Joey could even go for a
ride before bed.
Until Friday, yours truly,

Callie

Mase's first reaction was anger. He looked up from
the card and felt his jaw tense. That thing about getting
Joey on a horse again. She wasn't going to leave it
alone. Did Miss Callie Thorne think she was being sub-
tle? Well, he saw right through to the implication that
Joey needed therapy, and he couldn't help being
steamed. There wasn't a thing wrong with Joey that
time wouldn't heal. What a pushy female.

"Something wrong?" Luke asked.

Mase sighed. "No. It's nothing," he said. "Just
some chick I met."

"Women," Luke said with a ton of meaning.

"Yeah, women," Mase concurred, and an image of

Callie flew into his mind, the big hazel eyes and the wide, sensual mouth, the curtain of fine golden hair that hung to her shoulders. He saw her in an isolated moment of time, her slim fingers hooking a strand of silky hair behind a shell-pink ear, the flush on her cheeks...

Damn, he thought, confused. Here he was ticked at her for mentioning Joey, when he so desperately needed her. Her ranch, anyway. He hated that. Hated having to keep the stupid date and hated the dependence he felt. Frustration gnawed at him. Frustration with Callie and frustration with the Hitman—if only they'd find Hank Berry and lock him up. It was killing Mase that he'd had the man right there, right in his grasp, and he hadn't even known it. So now Metcalf was trying to shut Mase up. Killing a cop was bad news, so Berry had obviously been ordered by Metcalf to take the next best route: threatening Mase's son.

And hell, Mase thought, it was working. He was worried sick about his boy.

Mase hardly uttered a word as he and Luke drove to the north Denver park.

"You gonna sit in the car all day, LeBow?" Luke asked once they'd arrived and Mase still sat silently, lost in thought.

"Be right with you," Mase said, and forced himself to focus his attention on last night's drive-by shooting.

He went through the motions, ducked under the yellow crime-scene tape, took out his notebook, scribbled in it. Investigating murder really was despicable work, and even before Amy's accident, Mase had been thinking about quitting homicide. He still loved police work, but not the violence, not having to stare into the lifeless face of a victim, day after day after day. Vice would be better—anything would be better. The trouble was,

Denver was a big city now. With big-city problems and crime. When Mase had been a kid growing up here, crime seemed to be reserved for New York or L.A. or Chicago. Not anymore.

He and Luke did a thorough investigation of the area of the shooting, which had occurred near a child's swing set in the wee hours of the morning. Two night-shift uniformed policemen had done the preliminaries, the area had been photographed, and the body had been taken to the morgue. All that remained now was the white chalk outline of a fourteen-year-old kid in the dirt. And the only evidence they found—if it was evidence—was a crushed pack of cigarettes and three empty beer cans discarded nearby. As for footprints, the area had so many it was impossible to sort them out. Still, Mase called for several molds to be taken. He also had the swing set dusted for prints, but clearly it had been a drive-by shooting, and Mase was afraid the only way this case was going to be solved was if a witness came forward with information.

They took another hour that morning to knock on doors in the immediate vicinity of the park. Most folks were not home, and the few that were claimed they hadn't heard a thing. Mase listened, took names and a few notes, but he already knew he was wasting his time. Even if someone had witnessed the crime, he or she wasn't going to come forward. Too scared. It was hard to blame them.

Luke drove away from the neighborhood, and they stopped for lunch at a Mexican joint on Pecos Street, one of Luke's favorite spots. Over burritos, they discussed the case and a half-dozen others, open files on their desks. Mase had a hard time concentrating—he kept thinking about Joey and the ranch and just how he was going to arrange for his son to stay there until after the trial. He was pretty sure Callie Thorne wouldn't mind. But still, didn't he owe her an explanation? If he did come forward with the truth, would it put her in an awkward spot or, he shuddered to think, in danger?

"Man, you really are in left field," Luke said to him. "Is something up?"

"No, I was just thinking about this trip I have to make this weekend. A ranch up in Wyoming."

"The bachelor auction thing?"

Mase nodded then grimaced.

"You got bought," Luke stated, then he laughed. "Tell me. I wanna hear every last detail."

So Mase told him, and he couldn't help smiling and shaking his head when he described the Someday Ranch and Callie.

"It sounds as if the lady is doing some good work there," Luke said.

"Oh, she is. Her whole family is. No doubt about it. It's a good life. Clean. But Callie…"

"Go on."

"I don't know. She's a bit of a dreamer. Seems to think there's magical power or something to the ranch. Or maybe it's in the horses." Mase shrugged.

Luke cocked his head. "Or maybe it's something in the water."

Then they both laughed. When they were paying the check, Luke said, "So, all her flakiness aside, what do you really think about her?"

"What does it matter?" Mase replied.

"I don't know. Since last year, you know, when you lost Amy, well, you haven't even had a date."

Mase grunted. "You don't know that."

"Sure I do. And all I'm getting at is that it's not going to hurt you to let loose a little. You said she was pretty."

"I said she was a scrawny-cowgirl type with an interesting face," Mase countered.

"Yeah, well, *is* she pretty?"

"I suppose she is," Mase allowed.

"So, the weekend could be fun."

"I've got other things on my mind," Mase quickly reminded his partner.

"The trial."

"Yeah, the trial. And I can't be dinging around the Wyoming hills with some cowgirl and concentrating on the trial at the same time."

"The FBI got any word on the Hitman yet?"

Mase frowned. "Not a damn thing."

"They'll nab him eventually."

"Yeah," Mase said, leaving out the real thought running like a broken record through his brain. They'd nab Berry, all right, but it might be too late. Suddenly the bean-and-beef burrito felt like lead in his gut.

They stopped back at headquarters and filed their first reports on the crime scene. Paperwork and more paperwork. Then they reviewed two other open-file cases they were assigned to and revisited one of the crime scenes out in the suburb of Englewood. After that it was across town to yet another murder scene at a drive-through liquor store. By the time they finished it was past five. Mase used his cell phone to check on Joey and to let his folks know he'd be late picking up his boy.

"Don't you worry," Brenda told him, "Joey's fine. He and your dad are out back playing catch."

"Was Joey okay today?" Mase asked.

There was a pause, then his mother said, "He was awfully quiet most of the day."

Mase could hear it in her voice, the concern, even the pity. He just couldn't take it. His own mother. Pitying him, pitying Joey. He felt as if his life were spinning out of control.

In the car, on the way back to headquarters, Luke told him he thought it was time Mase had a break. "Man, go to Wyoming. Relax. I can't stand to see you so bummed out."

Mase shut his eyes for a moment. "I do need a break, Luke, you're right. And a lot of it is this work."

"Homicide?"

"Yeah," Mase said, "I think I'm heading for burnout. It's not just losing Amy, and it isn't having to care for my boy all by myself now. Hell, my folks have him a lot. It really is the job. I'm sick of it and my head's all messed up. Even the captain recognizes it."

"So what are you going to do?" Luke asked.

"Damned if I know" was all Mase could say.

CHAPTER FIVE

CALLIE WALKED ACROSS the dew-touched grass Friday morning to collect the horses she needed, four halters over her shoulder, carrots in hand, muttering to herself the whole time so that even the horses looked askance at her.

"Oh, brother," she said as she haltered Milky Way, "how'd I get myself into this?"

She was a jumble of nerves. Mase and Joey were due at the ranch in—she checked her watch—in ten, twelve hours. Less? "Oh, man."

She offered a carrot to Einstein and haltered him, then told him all about it. "He's a tough cop, and he doesn't give two hoots about me. He doesn't even care about Joey needing help."

Kahlua walked right up to her and took the carrot, and Callie slipped the halter over her head. Here she'd been dumb enough to think fate had directed Mase and Joey to the ranch, but it was all bunk, another one of her fantasies. She loved her fantasy world, but sometimes it would be nice to have something *real* happen.

She grabbed the black pony, Cinderella, and led all four back toward the barn, still muttering.

"Who are you talking to?" Jarod asked when she led the horses up.

"No one."

"You are really losing it," he said, shaking his head. "That's the first sign, you know, talking to yourself."

Callie shot him a warning look, then went on about her business, grooming the horses.

Would Mase leave work early because it was Friday? Or would he arrive late, because he didn't want to spend any more time here than he had to?

She could sense he didn't really want her company, and he sure didn't want Joey to ride. Heck, she could tell he didn't even like horses, and she'd let him off the hook about the date thing.

So why was he coming?

When she finally had the horses all ready to be saddled, she was still mumbling.

"So," she murmured to Cinderella, "do you think he's coming back out of a sense of honor?"

Then, to Milky Way, she said, "Maybe he just likes my dad."

Slipping the halter off Einstein, the big gray gelding, she wondered, "Or does he need some R and R?"

And finally, to Kahlua, she said, "What do I care, anyway? Just why the heck do I care, girl?"

All day as she worked, as she went through the exercises with her patients, as she laughed with them, encouraged them, taught them new skills, a part of her mind waited with a kind of tense expectation. She found her eyes straying often to the long ranch road, anticipating his car arriving, a plume of dust behind it.

After lunch she worked with Peter. His problem was somewhat different from the others; he had no neurological injury, but his brain fired too rapidly. It affected his concentration and his coordination, and the exercises helped him focus. The horse and its movement calmed him.

He was a kick, though, smart and quick, totally hyper all the time. If he became irritating, which could happen, everyone had learned to distract him or gently remind him to slow down. Callie was convinced that he really did "see" things, and that it was a result of the unique way his brain was wired.

In most therapy sessions there were three walkers, one person to lead the horse and one on each side, supporting the rider's legs. It was labor-intensive therapy, and Callie, who was usually a side-walker so she could direct the exercises, was always short of help. On weekends she got volunteers from Lightning Creek, but weekdays were hard.

Luckily, some of her patients didn't need as much physical support. Like Peter.

"Can I trot, can I trot?" he asked. "I feel good today, I want to trot."

"Maybe later. Let's work on raising your arms. That's it. Keep 'em up. Feel the horse walking. Roll with it. Now we'll stop and you swing your legs over. Sit sideways, Peter. You know the routine. We're walking again. Now backward. Okay, good. See if you can hold your hands up again. We're walking, we're walking. Good job."

She did let Peter trot Cinderella around the ring. All alone. He was thrilled, his face aglow. When he got off the pony, Callie hugged him, and truly, for a moment, she forgot all about Mase LeBow.

Then she noticed Rebecca, nearly hidden behind the fence surrounding the ring. That beautiful, solemn face.

"Hi, Rebecca," Callie said. "Is it your turn now?"

Of course, the little girl didn't answer. Silently, she entered the ring, holding the required hard hat. She knew the routine by now, but she merely went through the motions. The only thing that reached her was the horses; she loved them.

It was a hot afternoon, and by three o'clock, Callie was dry and dusty and tired. Off to the west behind the hills, thunderclouds were building, an afternoon rainstorm on its way. It was a common-enough occurrence in Wyoming. Callie figured she'd get the last therapy session in before the deluge. It was James, a man of sixty who'd suffered a stroke. He'd been at the ranch for almost two months now and was coming along really well, with only a slight limp now. Jarod would help her with him as a safety precaution.

The session went well, but by the time it was over, the wind had picked up, swirling dust devils across the riding ring. By five the sun was hidden and distant thunder growled. Then came the first big drops, splashing on the dry ground, and everyone still outside grabbed the horses and scampered inside the barn to wait out the storm.

It was over in twenty minutes. Everyone emerged from the barn to find the sun out, the air washed clean, the trees looking refreshed.

And Mase LeBow's blue Jeep Cherokee driving up the ranch road.

"Well, well," Jarod said, "here's your date, Callie."

"Be quiet, Jarod," she growled.

She stood there, holding Kahlua and Cinderella by the reins, her oldest jeans on. She felt dusty and sweaty, and her hair hung limply, damp tendrils escaping the rubber band that held it back. She glanced down at her cowboy boots. They were so old the toes curled up like Persian slippers. Oh, yes, she was ready for a date, all right.

Mase got out of the car, stretched his back and looked around. Joey popped out of the passenger side, stood there for a minute then spied Callie. More important, he saw Kahlua and ran over to smile up at her.

"Hello," he said to the horse.

Kahlua twitched her ears meaningfully. Joey dug in his jeans pocket and came up with a dirty, crumbling lump of sugar. He held it out to her, and she lipped it up.

"Hey, Joey," Callie said, "that was a really nice thing you did. She's been working all day, you know."

"Uh-huh."

Mase strode up then, slowly taking off his sunglasses as he got to Callie.

"Hi there, Mr. LeBow," Jarod said.

"It's Mase, please."

"Sure thing. Good to see you back."

"Thanks, Jarod." He turned his gaze on Callie. "Well, we're here," he said.

"So I see. Did you get hit by the rain?"

"Sure did. Slowed me down some."

Small talk. Absurd, foolish.

But Mase didn't look small or foolish or any such thing. He looked downright handsome. He was wearing khakis and a salmon-colored polo shirt, which made him seem more tanned than she recalled. His blue eyes were clear and alert, his hair full, dark, that lock falling softly on his brow. He was taller than she remembered, too, taller and perhaps trimmer, fit-looking. No doughnut breaks for Detective LeBow.

Callie cleared her throat, acutely aware of how bad she looked in comparison—the sweat, grime, stringy hair. "So, you're here," she said, dragging her eyes up to his. "I'll get someone to show you where you're staying. One of the guest rooms in the house. Do you think Joey would rather stay with the kids in one of the bunkhouses or with you?''

No hesitation. ''Better put him with me.''

''Sure, okay. Mom's got the room ready.'' She shuffled her old boots in the rain-damp earth. ''Let me just put the horses in the paddock there, okay?''

Walking ahead of him to the house, Callie wondered if the seat of her threadbare jeans was intact. She hoped so.

The house was cool and filled with the aromas of food cooking. And something baking. Francine was hard at work.

''Welcome, Mase—where's Joey?'' Liz asked as she emerged from the kitchen.

''Out with the horses,'' Callie answered. ''Can you get Mase settled while I finish up outside?''

''Sure. Come on, I'll show you your room,'' her mother said, and Callie gratefully escaped.

Once the horses were taken care of, Callie found time to take a long, hot shower, put a quart of body-building conditioner in her hair, and dress in a new pair of jeans, a round-necked pink T-shirt and sandals. Formal dinnerwear.

Mascara, pale-pink lipstick. No blush. Heaven forbid. Callie had enough natural blush. And why in blazes was she putting on makeup, anyway?

Dinner was the usual noisy, cheerful occasion. Mase seemed to turn into a different guy with the other men around. He regaled them with cop stories, had them guffawing or listening closely, pretty darn impressed.

Then Jarod asked him about his years at the Lost Springs Ranch, and he told them, quite matter-of-factly, about his terrible teens and how he put his folks through hell.

"Think Joey will put you through the same kind of hell?" Tom asked.

"Boy, I sure hope not." Mase looked down the table at his son, who was sitting between Sylvia and little Rebecca. Then he shook his head. "It gives me gray hairs, I'll tell you."

Liz studied him. "I don't see any gray hairs."

"Figurative gray hairs," Mase said, and he smiled at Liz. Actually smiled, for goodness' sake.

Callie was much too aware of Mase sitting next to her. His tanned muscular forearm lay on the table next to hers, and she couldn't help noticing the contrast between the silver of the watch he was wearing and the golden tan of that arm. She saw, too, that the short, crisp hairs on his forearm were practically the color of honey.

"More potatoes?" someone said, and Callie took the bowl and passed it along, tearing her gaze away from the arm that lay so close to hers.

Mase seemed perfectly at ease with the rowdy group, but he kept his attention on others, never on her. Frankly, she was getting sick of being ignored.

"Mase," she said, realizing she was deliberately throwing down the gauntlet to get his attention, "how about we give Joey a ride on Kahlua tomorrow?"

He turned to her, surprised for a moment, then his jaw tightened, and his voice turned cool. "I don't trust horses. They can be dangerous, and I don't think Joey needs to be put at risk."

"Our horses aren't dangerous," she said mildly. "And I think it would be a wonderful experience. We take all the safety precautions there are."

"I don't know what you expect to accomplish," Mase replied. "Joey doesn't need your therapy or your pity."

She was taken aback by his defensiveness. "Sorry, it was just an idea," she said in a huff. So much for good intentions.

Her dad, not hearing the exchange, took the opportunity to invite Mase along on a horseback ride the next day. He and Peter and Jarod were going on a trail ride.

"Thanks," Mase said tightly, "but I'm really more the touch-football type."

Callie was glad to help wash dishes after dinner; it absolved her of having to be around Mase. She was sure he was just as relieved. She pulled on yellow rubber gloves and scrubbed away at the pots. As she worked, she couldn't help wondering again why Mase had come back to Wyoming. And then she thought about his marriage and his wife and how sad it all was, and how much Joey must miss his mother, and when her eyes filled with tears, she pretended she'd gotten soap in them.

The dishes were done eventually, and there was no escape. In the living room, with its deep comfortable chairs, worn Oriental rugs and white wainscoting, Callie thought about excusing herself, saying she was tired and had to get to bed, but her mother foiled her plans.

"So," Liz said, "aren't you two supposed to be on a date? What kind of date is this?"

"Mom, I don't think…"

"Mrs. Thorne, I really don't…"

They spoke at the same time, then stopped and started over. "I'm okay right here," Mase began, and Callie chimed in, "I'm really sleepy." She yawned for good measure.

"Listen to that, will you?" Tom said. "You'd think they were old fuddy-duddies like us."

"What's there to do, anyway?" Jarod asked. The only place he ever frequented was the Roadkill Grill, which opened its saloon bar at 8:00 p.m.

"How about a movie?" Francine suggested.

"A movie," Callie repeated.

"Sure, at the Isis Theater. You know what's playing?" the red-haired cook asked.

"Now, wait a minute," Callie said. "Maybe Mase doesn't like movies."

Tom was rattling the local paper, looking for the movie schedule.

"I don't mind movies, but isn't it kind of late?" Mase suggested.

Francine shook her head. "There's a nine o'clock show." Then she grinned wickedly.

"Here it is," Tom said, "*The English Patient*. Seen it?"

"No," Callie said.

"No," Mase said.

"Well then, there you are."

"That's an old movie, isn't it?" James remarked. "It came out a couple of years ago."

"Well, the Isis gets things late," Sylvia explained. "About the time they come out in video. The owner's too cheap to pay for first-run films."

"Dom isn't cheap," Liz protested. "There's just not enough of a market here, Sylvia."

"Mase, be honest, do you want to see *The English Patient?*" Callie asked.

He looked around the room as if trapped, then his gaze fell on Joey.

"Don't worry about Joey," Sylvia said. "We'll take

real good care of him. And look, he's playing with Rebecca. Isn't that cute? They're coloring.''

They were indeed. The two youngest on the ranch were squatting over coloring books, choosing colors with great deliberation, each checking out whether the other was staying in the lines.

"Oh, go on, you two. Live a little," Francine urged them.

"Thorne out on a date." Jarod chortled. "What a kick."

"Well, I guess," Mase said reluctantly. "I mean, if you don't mind..."

"I'd sure go," Marianne piped up.

"No more excuses," Hal added.

Callie looked at Mase; he gave a slight shrug, his expression neutral. How embarrassing, how awful. "Are you sure?" she asked weakly.

"Oh, be quiet and go," Sylvia said.

So that was how Callie found herself sitting next to Mase in his car as he drove into Lightning Creek.

"My speed too slow for you?" he asked pointedly.

"No, it's perfect. Honestly." She squirmed in her seat, feeling prickly all over. Luckily, the dark hid her heated cheeks.

"You probably hate movies," she eventually said, to break the uncomfortable silence.

"Not at all."

"Bet you don't like *The English Patient*."

"Never saw it, so I don't know."

"It's a love story. A chick flick. It's probably corny."

"Would you rather not go?"

"Oh, no, no, it's fine with me."

Sitting next to him in the funky little theater

crammed with every young person in town was even worse than she'd imagined. Their arms touched. When he crossed his leg, it brushed her thigh, so he quickly uncrossed it.

What was wrong with her? Callie liked men, she loved dates, loved going out. She even loved movies, especially romantic ones. So what was making her heart pound and her mouth dry?

When the love scene came between Ralph Fiennes and Kristin Scott Thomas, it was not as explicit as in so many modern movies, but much more moving.

"You want my handkerchief?" Mase whispered into her ear.

She must have been sniffing too loudly. "No," she whispered back. "I'm okay."

But she wasn't. As the movie grew even more tragic, tears ran down her cheeks. Finally, Mase put his handkerchief in her hand, closing her fingers around it. "Take it," he said, and she did.

The hankie was soaked by the time the movie was over, and Mase was apparently at a loss. He patted Callie's hand tentatively, then the lights in the theater came on. Callie felt stunned for a moment. Then she blew her nose hard into Mase's hankie and took a deep breath.

"You okay?" he asked. "I thought there for a minute…"

"Oh, yes, I'm great. I loved that movie. Did you?"

"It was a very good movie."

"Yes, it was." Then she realized she was holding his sodden handkerchief balled up in her hand. She looked at it, looked up at him. "Oh, my gosh, I'm sorry. I'll…I'll put it in the laundry at home. I'll…"

"Don't worry about it, Callie. I have others."

They stood and filed out of the theater, following dozens of red-eyed high school girls. The night was dark and cool, and Callie was grateful that her own tear-swollen eyes were hidden.

"I must look a sight," she said, surreptitiously wiping a finger below her eyes in case she'd wept black mascara smudges.

"You look fine."

"You can't see me in this light."

"Well then, we could check you out in better light."

"No, that's okay," she said quickly.

Mase stood looking down at her, his face shadowed. He had his hands in the pockets of his khakis. "Well," he finally said, "since this is a date, we should go somewhere. Maybe have a beer or something."

"Would you mind ice cream instead?" Callie asked. "The Roadkill Grill…"

"The what?"

"You know, the Main Street Grill. But people haven't called it that for ages. You must remember its great sundaes. And if you want a beer, you could get one there, too."

"Ice cream sounds good, to tell the truth."

Callie ordered her usual, the triple-scoop banana split with hot fudge, caramel and strawberry toppings. And whipped cream. Mase gaped when it arrived. A small bowl of vanilla ice cream with fudge sauce was set down in front of him. Callie raised her spoon and took a moment deciding which end to start at, when she realized Mase was staring at her.

"Oh," she said, "you want to try some? We can share if you want.…"

He shook his head. "How do you do it?"

"Do what?"

"Eat so much and stay so skinny."

She raised her shoulders, then lowered them again. "Just lucky, I guess." Then she dived into the fudge-covered end.

By the time she'd finished her banana split, raised voices were coming from the bar section of the restaurant.

Mase heard the fracas, too. Probably his cop instincts were itching to go investigate, Callie thought. He looked as if he wanted to stride right in there.

But he was saved from his sworn duty by the appearance of Sheriff Reese Hatcher, who had obviously been called by the bartender. His weathered face set, the sheriff sauntered through the café and disappeared inside the saloon. His quiet voice issued a warning, and the drinkers subsided.

"That was fast," Mase said.

"Oh, everyone knows Reese, and they know he won't stand for any fighting on his turf. He keeps a pretty tight lid on this town, well, on the whole county."

"Maybe we should recruit him for the Denver police force," Mase said dryly.

But Callie shook her head. "There's no way. Reese has been trying to retire for ages."

The sheriff finally came out of the barroom.

"Hi, Sheriff Hatcher," Callie said.

"Well, hello there, Miss Callie." He grinned, and his stern expression changed completely. He looked at her with such affection he could have been her grandfather.

"Sheriff, this is…"

"Oh, I know who he is. He's the Denver cop I gave a speeding ticket to. Yeah, right. Mason…Mason…"

Mase stood up, reached out his hand. "Mase LeBow."

"Nice to meet you, son," the sheriff said, shaking hands with Mase as if they'd never met before.

"What was going on in there?" Callie asked.

"Oh, the usual. You know, coupla young bucks feeling rowdy. Jerry Lawton and Mikey Scott."

"Oh, them."

"Yeah, them."

"You in a hurry, Sheriff?" Mase asked.

"Hell no. Only got duty till midnight. Nothing going on."

"Maybe you'd like to sit down for a few minutes and we'll compare notes about law enforcement," Mase said.

Callie looked at him, eyebrows raised.

"Wouldn't mind that a bit." Hatcher lowered his big frame onto a chair. He looked around for the waitress, saw her, raised a hand and nodded. The waitress nodded back.

Over coffee, the sheriff and Mase talked. Big-city versus small-town law enforcement. Callie listened, interested, but she wasn't really involved in the conversation. It was as if two neurosurgeons were talking in front of a layman.

"Well, we got problems here, too. Small town, you know every last soul," Hatcher was saying. "Now, how am I gonna pull in Katy Mercer's only son for drunk drivin' when I know he's the only way poor Katy gets around? I was raised with these folk, and I have a hard time causing 'em more pain."

"You at least have hope here, though," Mase countered. "I see so many young kids, and I know they're going to be dead before they're twenty. Drugs, guns, no life at all. No way to reach them.''

"I read about it in the papers,'' Hatcher said, "and that's about as close to it as I wanna get.''

"Yeah, me too, sometimes,'' Mase agreed.

"So—'' Hatcher gave Mase a look from under bristly gray brows "—what's a big-city fella like you doing here? You still here or you back again?'' His gaze switched to Callie, and there was blatant curiosity in it.

"Oh, I'm staying at the Thornes' ranch. You know, that bachelor auction thing.''

Hatcher peered closely at Mase. "You're one of those boys from Lost Springs Ranch?''

"I sure am.''

"I knew you looked familiar.''

"Were you sheriff back then?'' Mase asked, surprised. "Twenty years ago?''

"Always been sheriff here,'' Hatcher said. "So, Callie, is this the guy you bid on?''

"Yes, this is him.''

"Not bad for a city fella,'' Hatcher allowed.

Mase grinned. How come, Callie thought, he never grinned like that at her? Male bonding was fine and good, but why couldn't Mase be pleasant to her, too?

The sheriff leaned across the table and spoke quietly to Mase. "You know that speeding ticket I gave you?''

"Oh, yeah, I sure do.''

"Well, I haven't sent it in to the state yet. It might just get changed to a warning.''

"That's not necessary, Sheriff. I *was* speeding.''

"Don't be so damn honorable, son.'' Hatcher laughed. "I am a mean old son of a gun sometimes. Mighta had some indigestion that evening.''

"Well, thanks," Mase said.

"Gotta go. Nice talking to you." Hatcher stood, put a finger to the brim of his Stetson and clumped out of the restaurant.

On the ride home, Callie was very quiet. She'd seen many sides to Mase LeBow: father, widower, policeman, one of the boys. But to her he was always the same—cool, withdrawn, almost defensive. He simply didn't like her. Well, maybe he didn't actively dislike her, but she obviously wasn't his type.

She pondered that. She'd tried her darnedest to let him off the hook about their dumb date. Why had he driven all the way up here, three hundred miles, to be with someone he couldn't care less about?

Her hands were in her pockets and her fingers closed around the damp hankie. She couldn't help remembering the way his hand had closed over hers in the theater and the warmth of his touch. She shivered a little then, glad her face was hidden from him in the dark interior of his car.

How silly, Callie mused, to be so sentimental over an old hankie.

CHAPTER SIX

JOEY WOKE MASE BRIGHT and early the next morning. "Daddy, I already had breakfast, and Sylvia told me to ask you if I could go out and play."

"What…" Mase mumbled, half-asleep, an arm flung over his eyes.

"Can I?"

"Sure."

"Okay, Daddy." And he was gone, his shoelaces untied, yesterday's grubby T-shirt back on.

Mase lay there in the guest room, the sun pouring in the window, and it suddenly hit him as his brain came fully awake that Joey wasn't clinging to him anymore; he'd gotten up by himself, dressed, eaten breakfast and made plans. All by himself. *This is good,* Mase told himself. *Very, very good.* And yet, deep in a corner of his mind, there was a minuscule ember of resentment, well, almost jealousy—all of a sudden Joey didn't need his old dad anymore. Okay, maybe they'd had a dysfunctional dependence on each other since Amy had died. Joey's counselor had hinted at that. But who else did Joey have now? His grandparents, sure, but Mase was his father.

He doused that pernicious little ember with the cold water of reason. It was definitely good for Joey to become independent. Absolutely terrific.

He got up and showered and realized he felt great.

Joey was safe and he had the whole day ahead of him with nothing to do, no life-or-death decisions to make, no killers to deal with. A vacation.

He thought about last night as he shaved and trimmed his mustache. It had been a surprisingly good movie. A study of passion. Tragic passion. Callie had sobbed so hard he wondered if she'd seen most of the film. He shook his head, smiling. Her eyes had been red and swollen, her nose shiny, and there had been mascara half-moons beneath her lower lids. She'd been appealing, anyway, her face scrubbed clean like a kid's, her pretty pink lipstick chewed off her wide, curvaceous lips.

And, boy, could she put away ice cream.

He splashed his face with water, cleaned his razor and dressed in jeans and a Police Athletic League T-shirt.

The ranch was bustling. There was a buffet breakfast set up in the dining room, and Hal and Marianne were just finishing their meal. Linda, another guest, sat at the table in a wheelchair.

"Good morning," she greeted him. "I'd recommend the scrambled eggs—they have ham and mushrooms in them."

"Sounds great."

Mase ate a much bigger breakfast than he was used to, but it was a good thing, he found out later. When he headed outside, he was greeted by a scene of controlled mayhem. Several cars and trucks were drawn up by the barn, one of them Sheriff Hatcher's Blazer. Callie and Jarod were walking a horse around in the ring, and on its back was a little girl of seven or eight wearing thick glasses. She was giggling as she performed certain movements on the horse's back. He could hear Callie's voice, encouraging, praising. Was this playing therapy?

Reese Hatcher was standing by the fence of the riding ring watching, one foot up on a rail. From the barn's open door Mase could hear people talking and horses whinnying. A regular circus.

"Good morning," Mase said, moving up to stand next to the sheriff. "I didn't expect to see you here."

"Oh, yeah, some of us come out from town on Saturdays to help out. Volunteers. Callie needs a lot of help with some of her patients. It's a good cause."

"Do you need to be trained to do it?"

"Nah, just common sense. Callie does all the technical stuff. I'm a side-walker. I walk next to the horse and hold on to the rider's leg to steady 'em—for the ones that need that."

"So, what's she doing with this little girl?"

"That's Mary Hardaway's daughter Emmy. She was born real premature, has some coordination problems. Boy, has she improved, though. Mary brings her out once a week. You know, she's been coming since she was a little bitty thing. Took her first step after she got off a horse. It was something to see."

Mase watched the session in the ring. Around and around the pony went, while Callie instructed the little girl with her exercises. They all seemed to be having so darn much fun. Mase quickly grasped what was going on. Before his eyes, the little girl was learning balance and muscle control. To sit on the moving horse, every muscle in her body had to adjust constantly.

When the session was over, Emmy was able to get off the pony by herself, sliding down onto the mounting block. She was so excited she jumped up and down, calling out to a lady who'd been watching. "Mommy! Did you see?"

"Yes, Emmy, I saw. You were wonderful," her mother called back.

Mase saw Callie bend down to say something to Emmy and then she hugged the girl, a great big hug, and Emmy hugged her back.

"See you next week," Callie called out to Emmy's mother. "She's doing great, Mary."

"Wonderful, isn't it?" Hatcher said.

"Seems to be."

"A real miracle is what it is," Hatcher insisted.

Mase went back to the house to check on Joey, a little nervous that he hadn't seen him in a while. The house seemed empty, but when he stuck his head in the fragrant kitchen, there was Joey, standing on a chair and mixing something in a bowl next to Rebecca, who stood on her own chair. They were dusted with white.

"They're kneading bread dough," Francine said.

"Good God, I hope he washed his hands," Mase replied.

"I did, Daddy."

"I'm very relieved to hear that." He turned to the petite cook. "Are they bothering you, Francine? I can take the kids and…"

"They're fine, Mr. LeBow," she said. "Good company."

"Well, okay."

"See, Rebecca," he heard Joey say, "I told you he'd let me."

As far as Mase could tell, Rebecca didn't answer, not in words, but Joey seemed to understand her as well as if she had spoken.

"You be good, kids," Mase said. "I'll be hanging around outside somewhere."

That "somewhere" proved to be the back forty on Tom Thorne's new tractor.

"Come on, I like company," Tom said. "Get away from all the commotion. Saturdays are nuts around here."

A fence line was down beyond the hay fields. Some horses had gotten out, and although they had been rounded up, it had taken a few days to find the break in the fence. Mase wasn't much help; all he could do was hand Tom tools. The wire was restrung, tightened and fastened to the fence post in short order.

"There," Tom said, standing with his hands on his hips, "that'll keep them in."

Then he rode in the big tractor with Tom as he picked up a huge complicated-looking attachment. They pulled it out to a hay field, recently cut and baled, where Tom drove down the rows and the attachment picked up bales on a kind of moving belt and stacked them neatly on a platform.

"Wow," Mase said.

"Easier than doing it by hand, huh?"

"Impressive."

"Expensive," Tom said. "I share it with some other ranchers around here. Next week it goes to Rich Metger."

When the platform was full, Tom drove back to the hay barn and unloaded the bales. This time Mase could help, directing Tom and piling up bales that fell. Farm work. Physical work, pure and simple. And when it was over, no worries, no danger, no death threats to his son hanging over his head. Not a bad life.

Lunch was another buffet-style meal, because everyone operated on different schedules. Mase ate too much again, but he'd worked hard that morning, physically hard. Callie came in to grab a bite as Mase was finishing a sandwich.

"I noticed that my dad had you working," she said.

"I warned you." She was hot and dusty, her cheeks flushed. Her blue tank top and jeans were worn—nicely, Mase thought—and there was a faint sunburn on her shoulders. She was slapping her wide-brimmed Stetson on her thigh as she spoke.

"I enjoyed it," he said.

Joey was squatting in a corner with Rebecca, and they were feeding Beavis and Butt-Head scraps from the lunch table.

"Is that okay?" Mase asked, gesturing to the kids.

"Sure, those dogs have garbage disposals for stomachs."

He watched Callie as she piled tuna salad and pickles, sprouts, tomatoes and lettuce on bread. She said something to her mom, then to Marianne, and they laughed together. She tousled Joey's head in passing, patted the mutts, had a word with James, then went and sat next to Linda at the long oak table and began to eat that huge Dagwood sandwich.

Mase got himself a refill of iced tea and sat on a couch. He had a view out the window, across the fields to the rising foothills. But if he turned his head a bit, he could see the dining room and the various guests eating lunch. He could also see Callie. She managed to eat and talk at the same time, and her hands made airy gestures to punctuate her speech.

He found himself studying her, watching those dancing expressions on her face. In a matter of seconds they changed from sympathy to humor to understanding to earnest caring. He saw the way wisps of her hair fell across her cheek and how she pushed them back with a slim wrist because her hands were holding the sandwich. He noted the smiles—genuine smiles—she bestowed on everyone within the circle of her radiance, as if she were a shining sun. Only Mase was in eclipse, untouched by her brightness.

Tom approached as Mase was finishing his iced tea and a brownie Francine had pressed on him. Slapping his own belt, Tom asked if Mase had eaten enough.

"I'd say so. Me and those dogs, we're stuffed," he replied.

"Oh, them." Tom turned and watched the kids make the mutts sit and shake hands for scraps. "It's good for 'em." He laughed when Beavis licked Joey's face. Rebecca smiled shyly.

"Guess Rebecca needed a kid her own age," Tom said. "But then again, maybe not just any kid woulda helped. Joey is a godsend. She's coming out of her shell with him around."

"Uh-huh," Mase said, wondering whether there really was something in the water on the Someday Ranch that made everyone so darn optimistic.

"How about a ride this afternoon?" Tom asked. "Jarod and I were talking about it."

"Oh, I don't think so. Like I said, horses and I don't get along. Maybe some other time."

"Sure, just let me know."

"Oh, I will." *Right,* he thought.

When Tom left, he noticed that Callie was staring his way. Probably wondering what he and her father were talking about. She swiftly glanced away, and he could see her cheeks flush. Why had she been watching him?

Well, hell, he could probably figure it out. She was wondering why on earth he'd come up here to bug her when she so obviously didn't care if she ever saw him again. The excuse that he wanted to keep their date was a lame one. She wasn't dumb, and she was probably getting suspicious. Why had Mase LeBow inflicted himself on her?

God, he wished he could tell her, just lay it all out on the line: "There's been a death threat against my son because of testimony I have to give in court, and I want him up here in the hills of Wyoming where he'll be safe." That's all he'd have to say, and he knew Callie wouldn't give a darn about how much she disliked the father—she'd take in the son without a peep. And she'd protect him and love him just as she did everyone on the ranch.

But, of course, he couldn't tell her.

And she'd continue to watch him with doubt and distrust in her wide hazel eyes, and that bothered him a lot more than it should have.

After lunch, Callie asked Mase if it was all right if Joey came out to the barn with her. He and Rebecca could be a lot of help getting the horses ready; it was going to be a full afternoon.

"Sure," he said, "as long as he's not in the way."

"Goodness, no," she said, then she went over and leaned down to talk to the two kids. In a second they were following her outside, and Joey was skipping with excitement. Just as they went through the front door, Callie reached for Joey's hand, and without hesitation he took it. Rebecca took Joey's other hand, and they looked so much like a mom and her kids that Mase felt something tighten in his chest.

"Cute, aren't they?" Tom asked.

"Yeah. Joey's having a ball."

"Well, now that's taken care of, and if you don't have anything else to do, I was wondering if you'd like to go into town with me. To the feed store. Jarod's busy with patients, and I could use some help loading the feed bags."

"I'd be glad to," Mase said.

It was a pleasant drive. The windows of the pickup were open and a cool breeze blew Mase's hair around. Tom was easy to be with and talked idly of his family.

"Callie's older brother lives in Jackson Hole. He's got two kids, wonderful kids. Only thing is, me and Liz don't get to see them enough, we're so busy. It's easier in winter, when everything slows down a lot, but then the weather's so bad I hate for any of us to be out on the roads. We manage to get together for Christmas, anyway.

"Callie's so dedicated to her work. Went all over the country taking courses in neuromuscular development and the special kind of therapy she does. She's very safety minded, too, takes all the precautions listed in the NARHA manual—that's the North American Riding for the Handicapped Association. Callie's got all the required helmets, saddles, wheelchair-accessible mounting blocks. That girl's a real stickler for rules." Tom glanced over at Mase. "We're pretty darn proud of her, but you know, we sorta wish she'd get out more. That was sure nice of you to take her to that movie last night. Girl her age needs more of that."

"It was my pleasure," Mase said.

"Was it, now?" Tom replied. "Looked more like a chore for both of you."

"Oh, no, not at all. Callie's a very nice girl. I enjoyed taking her out."

"Yeah, like you'd enjoy wrestling porcupines."

"Tom, honestly…"

"Oh, I know, Callie can be…well, I guess you'd say she's a little different."

"Yes, she is."

"Hey, don't think I'm trying to push her on you. My Callie has a mind of her own. I wouldn't interfere, not me."

Mase sat there, staring straight ahead. What was he supposed to say to that? He sifted through possible replies, but discarded every one. In the end he said nothing.

Reilly's Feed Store was right next to Twyla's Tease 'n' Tweeze and two doors down from the Roadkill Grill, where he and Callie had been last night. Tom drove around back and spoke to a broad-shouldered young kid. Soon the fifty-pound bags of grain for the horses were being tossed into the back of the truck by the three of them.

"Put it on my account, okay?" Tom said, and they drove back down Main Street and out of town. Tom seemed to wave to almost everyone they passed.

"Small town, you know everybody," he remarked to Mase.

"It's nice."

"It is, yeah, it sure is."

When they arrived at the ranch, Tom backed the truck up to the big barn doors, ready to unload the grain. Mase climbed out to help.

He didn't notice Joey at first, not with all the people standing around and the horses tied to the corral poles waiting to be ridden. His ear must have recognized Joey's voice over the din, though, because he walked around the pickup and searched the area for his son but couldn't see him.

Little Rebecca appeared silently at Mase's side and took his hand. He glanced down at her, surprised, and she tugged his hand. He went with her, and somewhere behind him he heard Tom say, "Will you look at that." He glanced to where Rebecca was leading him, and there, in the riding ring, was Joey, perched on a big brown horse and being led around the ring by Callie.

Joey saw him and grinned. He waved at his father and yelled, "Hey, look at me on the horse, Daddy!"

Rebecca pulled Mase closer, and he was right at the fence watching his son ride a horse—a happy little boy, an excited, joyous little boy.

Callie led the horse to the fence, her eyes met Mase's and held them for a moment, daring him to object. There was such fire in her gaze that he wouldn't have had the nerve to provoke Callie Thorne, not in a million years. In any case, Mase could not have gotten the words past the lump in his throat.

CHAPTER SEVEN

CALLIE LED KAHLUA BACK into the center of the ring, reminding Joey not to bounce around in his excitement. But even as she spoke, she was aware of Mase's gaze on her. She felt prickly hot, her skin supersensitive, as if she had a fever. She told herself over and over that she didn't care what Mase LeBow thought—putting Joey on the mare's back was the best thing that could have happened. She ached to turn, to cry out to Mase, "Look, look at your son, look how happy and alive he is," but she wisely kept her mouth clamped shut. If Mase couldn't see it, well, he was blind.

It struck her then, like a brick falling on her head, that this might be exactly why Mase had returned to the Someday Ranch. It wasn't to see her again, and it wasn't because he felt obligated to keep the date. He'd come back for Joey. Somehow, subconsciously, Mase had realized this was what his son needed.

Callie worked with Joey for another twenty minutes and then taught him how to slide off Kahlua's back onto the mounting block. Joey would have stayed on the mare all afternoon given half a chance, but Callie knew that even at his tender age, he would have one heck of a sore rear end in the morning.

"Down you go, Joey," she said, guiding him onto the block. "And now you can help Jarod give her some oats. Would you like that, pardner?"

Joey nodded eagerly. "Can Rebecca help, too?"

"Uh-huh," Callie said, "but you'll have to find her. I think I just saw her take off toward the house."

Joey raced off to find his new friend, totally bypassing Mase. Callie watched the boy's father, trying to gauge his reaction, but his expression was neutral.

She led Kahlua past him and into the barn, where she removed the mare's saddle and bridle and placed them in the tack room. "Phew," she said, turning, and there was Mase, right behind her, muscular arms folded across his chest, leaning a casual shoulder against the door frame. "Oh," Callie breathed, "you startled me." Inadvertently, she stepped back.

"Sorry," he said, his eyes on her. "I just wanted to say that was…amazing. Thank you."

They were so close, and the air was hot and heavy with the odor of hay and animal flesh. Callie felt suddenly breathless, unable to tear her gaze from his. He seemed bigger in the close quarters, bigger and stronger and curiously in charge. Sweat trickled down between her breasts as the moment stretched out, longer and longer.

After what seemed an eternity, Callie bit her lower lip and slid her stare away from his. Her brain churned frantically—what had he just said? Something about Joey? Yes, that must have been it. Mase had thanked her. *Wow.*

"You're welcome," she managed to say past the dryness in her throat. "I…I'm so glad you weren't mad—you know, about Joey riding and all. I…"

"It's all right," he said, still not moving, still filling the doorway. "I was an ass about it."

"Oh, no, no," she said quickly, despite the accuracy of his words. "You're just a protective father and that's good. Really." She looked up tentatively, and something flickered in his eyes, something she couldn't grasp. Anger? Regret? Lord, but she couldn't read this man, not one bit, and her stomach tightened in frustration. There was that dark side to him, dark and forbidding, and, oh, how she wanted to probe it. Had it started with the death of his wife? Or with his job? Had he been born with it already intact?

Callie shook herself mentally and forced a smile. "Hot in here," she said. "I'm ready for some lemonade. How about you?" She kept the smile on her lips and slipped past him.

Over lemonade on the porch, Callie ventured to bring up the subject of riding again. "So, you really don't ride, not ever?"

"Not if I can help it," Mase answered. He sat on the steps, his back presenting a formidable wall.

Then Joey appeared, the screen door banging behind him. "You could ride Kahlua, Daddy."

Mase was silent.

Even Tom, who was sitting next to Callie in a wicker chair, got into the discussion. "Diablo would be perfect for you," Callie's dad said.

Mase pivoted around. "Diablo?"

"It's a joke," Callie said. "Diablo is twenty-two years old and so sweet-tempered he won't take off if ten horses gallop right past him."

"Diablo," Mase grumbled.

"No, really," Callie said, "I'm not kidding. He's a dream." Then she grinned gave her father a wink. "I think you should ride Diablo."

Mase made no comment. He merely took a long drink of his lemonade and set the glass down on the step next to him, ice cubes tinkling.

"You still owe me a date," Callie said impishly. "I don't think baling hay with my dad qualifies." She turned to her father. "Do you think Mase has fulfilled his obligation?"

Tom shook his head. "Nope. I think Mase has done a darn good job of avoiding it."

Mase made a grunting noise.

Callie grinned wider. "You're right, Dad, he's been avoiding it like the plague. Now, I figure that I bought him with my hard-earned money, so I should get to choose the date."

Under his breath, Mase mumbled, "We went to the movies and then you stuffed down a banana split. That was your choice."

"Oh, no," Callie said, "the movie was *your* idea."

"Like hell it was," Mase said, but in the end, either out of humiliation or macho bravado or a sense of duty, he reluctantly agreed to the ride.

Because he'd only brought along his tennis shoes, Mase had to borrow a pair of Jarod's boots. While he tugged them on, Callie and her father saddled Diablo and Callie's mount, Satin Boy, a four-year-old quarter horse that her mom and dad had given her for her thirtieth birthday. Satin Boy was a delight, still young and frisky, and he ran like the wind as smoothly as any horse Callie had ever been on. He was a little hard to handle at times, especially if the weather was bad, but he was learning who was boss.

"Nice-looking horse," Mase said, the brim of his baseball cap tugged low and his hands on his hips as he surveyed Satin Boy. "You sure he isn't going to get old Diablo here all stirred up?"

"Nothing gets Diablo stirred up," Callie replied. But she would soon eat her words.

They mounted, then left the barn, heading north at a leisurely pace along a trail that wound up into the hills and onto a large grass and sage-dotted plateau beyond. Old Diablo, as promised, just plugged along, his big head down, swaying a little from side to side. Satin Boy, on the other hand, was raring to go, his smooth chestnut-colored flanks quivering beneath Callie and a sheen of sweat already glowing on his neck despite the slow pace. He kept throwing back his head, nostrils flared, and Callie scolded him with a touch of her knees and hands when he did a quick dance.

"If you want to run him," Mase said alongside her, "go ahead. We'll just keep plodding along here." He patted Diablo's mane. "Good ol' fella."

"I'll run him when I'm ready," Callie said. "He's still very young and has to learn who's riding who."

It was a beautiful late afternoon, storm clouds amassing far to the west and darkening the distant mountains. Bees buzzed in the tall grass, butterflies bobbed colorfully, and prairie dogs poked their heads from their holes as Callie and Mase passed. Overhead, an eagle wheeled on an ascending shaft of air, its huge wings spread effortlessly against the brilliant blue Wyoming sky. A fat whistle pig stood on its haunches on a boulder, nervously aware of the big bird.

Mase looked up. "Bald eagle?"

"Yep," Callie said, tipping her worn Stetson back to survey the sky.

"Do you ever spot golden eagles here?"

"Uh-huh. Can't miss them. Last spring there was one that had a ten-foot wing spread. I think he was nesting right up on that rock face." She pointed to the east, to a sheer, dry wall of reddish-brown rock that jutted out of the earth.

Mase rose up in his saddle, apparently trying to get a better view of the cliff.

And the words flew unbidden out of her mouth. "You don't have a bad seat," she said, eyeing Mase's firm jeans-clad rear end. Then, realizing she'd voiced aloud her thoughts, she quickly tried to qualify her statement. "I meant—I mean—you sit a horse okay." Her cheeks flamed.

Mase pivoted in the saddle. "I thought that's what you meant."

They rode for some time in companionable silence, enjoying the warm, dry air, the wide-open spaces. The light was changing, taking on that golden late-day glow, and it touched Mase's hair beneath the baseball cap and lit it softly, richly.

At one point Callie said, "This is nice, huh?" and Mase nodded.

She finally let Satin Boy have his head, leaving Mase in the dust as the gelding took off across the prairie, his neck flattened, his gallop flowing as smooth as silk beneath her. She let him fly until she was nearly to the base of the red cliff, and then she turned him, took him down into a canter, then a trot, and finally slowed him to a cooling-off walk as she headed back toward Mase.

She was exhilarated. Alive. She was always on a high when she rode, the hot, dry wind in her face and hair, the smooth muscles of a horse bunching and stretching beneath her, the heavy solid thud of hooves on the parched earth. The huge mass of the animal between her thighs, that unique horseflesh smell, the dust on her cheeks and hands, the sweat of her brow mingling with the horse's—it was all as utterly sensual to Callie as intimacy with a man. And today she felt giddy with life, her body expectant, all her senses in heightened awareness.

Mase was just up ahead now, moving toward her on Diablo. He might never ride, Callie mused, but he sure could sit a horse. She imagined Mase would look natural in any athletic endeavor—he simply had a great, well-tuned body. She guessed she'd known that from the very first, from the moment she'd laid eyes on him at the auction. Despite the menacing look, despite that dark, hidden side, Detective Mase LeBow had a body to die for.

Callie caught herself and immediately squelched the thought. Was she crazy? This was a silly arranged date. Period. Not a darn thing was going to come of it.

She had one of her visions then, blocking out the sage-dotted plateau, blocking out the heat, everything.

She was on a huge, colorful balloon, rising up into the sky. Suddenly an arrow pierced the balloon and it started to deflate, spinning out of control, crashing toward earth....

"You certainly can ride," Callie heard someone say, and she blinked. Mase. Somehow she had reached Mase again. "That was...beautiful, watching you like that."

"Thank you," Callie replied, and in spite of all the warning alarms sounding in her head, the balloon started to rise again.

It was a long ride back to the ranch. It wasn't late, but if they didn't pick up the pace a bit, dinner would be half over by the time they got home.

"Want to trot for a while?" she offered.

Mase shrugged. "Why not."

He did fine, and they made headway back toward the ranch. But Diablo tired quickly.

"The old boy here doesn't seem in too big a hurry," Mase said, and so they slowed down again. It was okay, Callie decided, because she had Mase's undivided attention.

"So where do you live in Denver?" she asked. "Downtown?"

"Bonnie Brae. Well, right on the outskirts. Little brick place."

"That's near...?"

"Cherry Creek. Sort of between there and Denver University."

"Shopping." Callie sighed. "Cherry Creek is such a nice area to shop in, or so I hear. It's the one thing I really do miss living in the sticks. Did your wife like to shop a lot?" Callie gave him a sidelong glance. Was she pushing?

But Mase didn't seem to mind. "Amy liked to shop, I guess." Then a tiny smile tugged at that mustached mouth. "Don't all women?"

"Oh, yes, at least everyone I know. So, if it's okay for me to ask, who takes Joey shopping—for clothes and things? I mean, since, well, since..."

"Amy died?" he cut in. "It's all right, Callie, I've come to terms with her death. It wasn't easy, but life goes on. And I've got Joey to think about. But to answer your question, my mother takes him shopping. She and Dad take Joey most everywhere, in fact. Dentist, doctor, you know."

Callie was listening, but mostly she was thinking that there didn't seem to be a special woman in Mase's life right now, at least not one close enough to help with Joey. She recalled her thoughts about what a local hero Mase must be with the big trial coming up and all that—not to mention his great looks—and she wondered why some gorgeous female hadn't snagged him.

"You, uh, don't have a friend to help look after Joey? I mean, well, when your folks are busy?"

Mase shot her a quick glance. "What sort of friend are you referring to?"

Darn him, Callie fumed. "You know, a lady friend, someone you go out with."

"No one," he said, "yet."

Yet. "Lindsay," she continued, "you remember Lindsay Duncan from the auction? Anyway, she mentioned you have some sort of big trial coming up in Denver."

There it was, that black cloud scudding across his face. She'd hit a nerve, but there was no way she was going to back off. "If you don't mind, could you tell me what you actually witnessed when…"

It came darting from behind a small scrub oak tree. If Callie had seen it in time… But she didn't. The jackrabbit flew right under Diablo's nose, startling the old boy, and he reared up and shied to the left at the same moment. Before Callie could grab the reins, Mase was losing his seat, sliding off to the right into a pile of rocks and…

Oops.

Callie was down in a flash, ground-tying Satin Boy and kneeling beside Mase. He had a hand on his forehead and…oh, goodness, blood was oozing out between his fingers.

"Mase? Mase, are you all right?" Callie breathed, on her knees beside him.

He groaned something, a few choice swearwords.

"Mase, let me take a look."

No way. She tried gently to pry his hand away from his forehead, but he resisted with a scowl.

"Mase, let me see it. Come on."

"I'm...fine. Just give me a minute."

He was not fine. Callie rose and unfastened the canteen from the clip on Diablo's saddle. She gave Diablo a disgusted look, and he hung his head in shame. "Stupid horse," she said, and she turned back to Mase. Squatting alongside him again, she yanked her tank top out of the waistband of her jeans and wet a corner of it.

"Let me at least clean off the cut," Callie said.

"I'm not cut."

"Oh, really? You better take a look at your hand, Mase."

That got him. He took his fingers away from his brow and eyed them numbly.

"See," Callie said, and she bent over him, carefully examining the wound. "I'm going to apply a little pressure. It may hurt a tad."

Mase was a terrible patient, a real baby. He let out a groan when she pressed the wet edge of her shirt to the cut and dabbed away the blood. The wound was oozing freely, like a typical head wound, but not gushing blood. It would clot in a couple of minutes.

Mase finally sat up, hunched over, legs crossed in the dirt. Callie was kneeling directly over him, holding her shirt up and away from her body as she used the hem to clean the wound. If Mase looked up... But he didn't.

It took a few minutes before the bleeding finally stopped, and Mase swore he was clearheaded enough to get to his feet.

Callie rose and helped him, tugging on an arm. "You might need a few stitches," she said.

"The hell with that," he muttered, and swayed against her.

"Whoa there," Callie said, placing an arm around his waist as he leaned on her. "I think you may have a concussion."

"I'm...okay," he breathed, but half his weight still rested on her and his arm remained around her shoulders. "Just give me another minute."

"Sure," Callie said, tightening her grip around his waist. At that moment she became aware of his body, the steel hardness of his narrow hips, the long muscles of his arm, heavy against her shoulders. She was acutely aware of his weight, the damp heat that emanated from him, the heady aroma of male sweat and dust and leather. She could see those crisp sun-bleached hairs on his forearm and the back of his sun-browned hand, the dark whisker shadow on his cheeks, the curve of his lips and nose. She could even smell the blood, metallic, coppery.

Something inside her tightened and shifted, and she felt the hard thud of her heart against her ribs. This wouldn't do, not at all, she was thinking, when another one of her crazy fantasies popped into her head.

She and Mase were alone, utterly alone in the desert, not unlike the desert in *The English Patient*. And Mase had been wounded by an enemy bullet. She got him to a cool cave and stripped him of his shirt. With a hankie wet with her own tears, she dabbed away at his blood, his sweat, her fingers tracing the lines of his chest, the sun-blond hairs, nurturing him, bringing him back to life. Days passed, and nights. Finally he sat up, and he brought her lips to his, kissing her deeply.

"You saved my life," he said. "You didn't leave me here to die."

He kissed her again and again, his mouth opening over hers....

"Ah," Mase groaned, his weight on her shoulder. "God, I feel stupid."

Callie forced herself back to reality, to Wyoming, the high prairie, to Mase and the cut on his head. *Wow.* she thought. *Some fantasy.*

"Can you walk?" she breathed.

"Uh, sure."

"Can you get back on Diablo?"

"Sure."

Callie led him toward the old horse, who was standing docilely a few feet away. "Are you sure you're okay? You can ride?"

"Fine, I'm fine," Mase said, and he removed his arm from her shoulder. "Whew." He leaned over and picked up his baseball cap from the dust. After slapping it against his leg, he put it on. Instantly, the cut began to ooze again.

Callie shook her head. "Here," she said, and she reached up and turned the cap so it sat on his head backward. "Well, you look like a high school kid, but I guess it's better than getting sunstroke."

"Am I still bleeding?" he asked.

She cocked her head. "No. Not really. But I'll sure feel better when we get home and clean that cut properly."

"It's fine," he repeated doggedly.

"Sure," Callie agreed, and she thought, *men.*

She helped him remount Diablo, and all the while Mase fussed that he was okay and didn't need any more help. She said nothing. He did seem better on the ride back, and she was relieved. Concussions were nothing to mess with. Still, she asked him a dozen times how his head was.

"I'm perfectly all right," he kept telling her, increasingly irritated.

When they were finally in sight of the barn, Callie said, "Mase, you aren't mad at Diablo, are you?"

"Of course not."

"But you're probably mad at me. I goaded you into this."

He reined Diablo in and turned to look at her. "No one goaded me into doing anything, Callie," he said tightly. "I'm a big boy. I enjoyed the ride. Most of it, anyway."

"I'm glad," she replied, dragging her gaze from the blue of his eyes. "We'll get that cut fixed up as soon as we…"

"Can I ask you a favor?" he interrupted.

She was ready to nudge Satin Boy but paused. "Sure. Anything. I sort of feel I owe you one."

"You don't owe me a thing," he said. "But I would appreciate it if Joey could stay on here for a while."

Callie was so taken aback that words failed her. She cocked her head at him in question. This was the last thing she'd expected.

"I'm maxed-out at work, and there's the trial coming up… My folks could use the break, too."

"Of course," Callie managed to reply.

"But if it's a problem…"

"Oh, no, no," she was quick to say. "We'd be delighted to have Joey."

"I'll pay for his keep."

"Mase…"

"I insist or it's off."

Callie shrugged. "Whatever."

"So he can stay?"

"Yes, I told you we'd be happy to have him."

"Good. Then it's settled."

"Sure. No problem."

"It's only for two weeks at the most, and I'll call every day."

"Not a good idea," she said. "What I mean is, the younger ones do much better if you give them time to adjust without calling. They get less homesick."

"You're sure?"

Callie nodded. "When Joey feels like it, we'll have him call you."

"I'll leave all my numbers—cell phone, pager, everything. Just in case."

She smiled. "He'll do great, and you aren't to worry."

Mase said, "I won't worry." But why, then, did he look so troubled?

They rode side by side to the barn, and the whole time Callie tried to make sense of it. Mase had been dead set against Joey getting therapy, but now he was apparently gung ho about it. What had happened? Was Mase that impressed with Joey's improvement after a single session? Somehow Callie doubted it. So what was going on? Was he really that tied up with the trial? she wondered.

She gave him a long look, trying to read him, trying to probe that worried expression, but he wasn't giving a hint as to his true motive. And then they were back at the barn, and Jarod and her dad were there, taking the horses' reins. They were alarmed at the dirt and blood on Mase's face and shirt, so there was no way Callie could question him any further.

Everyone fussed like mad over him. Joey clung to his leg again, frightened by the sight of blood on his father's face. Rebecca hid in a corner of the kitchen, and Liz, Francine and Sylvia hovered around Mase, who was embarrassed as all get out over the stir he was causing.

Callie watched the scene from the doorway. Francine was openly flirting with Mase like a big-eyed puppy, Sylvia was trying to play nurse, and Liz was directing everyone. "The first-aid kit's in the downstairs bathroom, and we'll need that new roll of adhesive tape from the bath upstairs...."

"Please," Mase was begging, "I'm fine."

"You should see a doctor," Liz said, and she went on about the seriousness of concussions. At one point Mase tried to smile at Callie as if to say he was dying a thousand deaths.

She kept staring at him, and she couldn't help recalling the feel of his hard body against hers, the male smell of him. Callie wasn't sure any man had ever had such an immediate and profound effect on her, yet Mase had done nothing to elicit such a wild response.

Joey was staying. She had dozens of questions about that. And yet one thing stood out as vitally important. If Joey remained here, then Mase was going to have to come back and pick him up. And that meant that Callie would see him again. She wasn't one bit certain how she felt about that. She was darn sure that nothing would come of it. And yet a part of her, a deep, secret part she rarely acknowledged, thrilled at the prospect— Mase was coming back.

CHAPTER EIGHT

MASE LEFT FOR DENVER after lunch on Sunday. Callie stood in the driveway holding Joey's hand and they both waved goodbye. She kept a close eye on Joey that afternoon, making sure he was occupied, watching for signs that he missed his dad. He was fine, though, playing with Rebecca, wrestling around on the lawn with Peter and the dogs, getting filthy. He fed Kahlua her grain and even helped Jarod turn the horses out to pasture after dinner that evening.

Joey moved into the bunkhouse where the guests stayed. He'd be with Hal and Peter and James and Jarod, so he would have plenty of company, and there would be adults to take care of any emergencies that might arise.

By Wednesday Joey had ridden Kahlua three more times; he'd even trotted, and was very proud of his progress. Rebecca was always present for his riding lessons, and Joey was there for hers. They were fast becoming inseparable. The funny thing was, Callie told Liz, Joey didn't seem to think it the least bit strange that his friend never spoke. He talked to her, and she seemed to communicate with him without words. Whatever it was, it worked.

By Wednesday evening, Callie noticed that Joey was quieter than usual and didn't take Hal up on his offer of a ride in his wheelchair, one of Joey's favorite pastimes. She took him aside and asked him what was wrong.

"Nothing," Joey said, trying hard to be brave.

"Do you feel okay?"

"Uh-huh."

"Are you a little homesick?"

Silence. Joey looked down at the scuffed toes of his white sneakers.

"It's all right to admit it, sweetie. Everyone gets homesick sometimes."

"Is my daddy coming back soon?"

"Well, he has to work. But you know he'll be back. I'm just not sure when." She paused. "Let's go give him a phone call, okay?"

Joey nodded, his face brightening.

Callie dialed Mase's number, and when it rang, she handed the phone to Joey. His eyes lit up when Mase answered. What must it be like, Callie wondered, to have a child whose eyes brightened like that at the sound of your voice.... She felt a stab of envy.

Joey's end of the conversation was brief: "Yes, Daddy. Fine. Three times, and I trotted. Yes. Hal lets me sit on his lap and we ride in the wheelchair. It's cool. Uh-huh. When are you coming?"

She could see he was a little crestfallen with Mase's answer. "Oh," Joey said, "okay. See you. Bye, Daddy."

On Thursday morning Jarod reported that Joey had cried during the night. Callie was concerned; her therapy couldn't cure homesickness.

"What should I do?" Callie asked her mom and Sylvia.

"Poor little tyke," Sylvia said. "It's probably the first time he's been away from home."

"I can't bother Mase with this. I know he's got an important trial coming up. He's probably working all hours." Callie paced the living room, one arm across her chest, the other propping up her chin.

"I'm getting an idea," her mother said, nodding sagely.

"What?"

"Well, if Mase can't come here, then you go there."

"Go to Denver?"

"You and Joey drive to Denver. Make it into a vacation for yourself. Shop till you drop. Go to first-run movies. Eat out. Dress up."

"Dress up," Callie said blankly.

"Well, at least wear a skirt."

"Mom, I can't. You know how busy we are."

"We'll handle everything here."

"I think you should," Sylvia agreed. "It's about time you got away from here. Go on, take a break. Go to the big city."

"I couldn't possibly," Callie protested.

"Ask Joey," Liz said.

Joey was all for the idea. He started running off to the bunkhouse to pack his bag.

"Hold on there, pardner. We can't go till tomorrow, and don't you think we better call your dad?"

"No," Joey said, his voice shrill with excitement. "Let's surprise him! I want to, please."

"Joey, it's not very good manners to just show up at somebody's house...."

"It's *my* house! I want you to see it, Callie. My room has model airplanes and dinosaurs. Please, Callie, please."

Finally she agreed. It probably wasn't a great idea to leave Mase in the dark, but frankly, she wasn't keen on making that call. She feared Mase's response would be less than enthusiastic, and, hey, she was a sucker for surprises.

They made the trip on Friday, driving down the ranch road in Callie's pickup right after breakfast. Joey was restless and excited at first, but by the time they were south of Casper on I-25, rolling along at a good clip, he settled down. Callie had the radio on a country-western station, and she sang along with the songs.

To tell the truth, she was as much on pins and needles as Joey. Maybe more. He was going home to see his dad; she was sailing into uncharted waters. What would Mase do when she showed up out of the blue? Would he be angry or uncomfortable or just plain cool, as if he didn't give a darn one way or the other that Callie Thorne had just driven three hundred miles to see him?

Well, she wasn't driving the three hundred miles to see him; she was doing it for Joey.

As she drove, she thought about Mase and wondered how the cut on his head was. She hoped he didn't have any lingering effects, dizziness or headaches or anything. Silly old Diablo. Dumb rabbit. Of course it would have to happen to Mase, who disliked horses, anyway.

They stopped for lunch in a café. Joey had a melted cheese sandwich and fries, and Callie had a burger and potato salad. Then she peeked at the dessert menu.

"Strawberry shortcake?" she asked Joey. "Hot fudge sundae? Cherry pie with ice cream?"

He looked at her with wide eyes.

"How about we share one?"

They got the sundae and two spoons, but Callie ate most of it.

"Don't tell your dad," she said. "He'll say it's un-healthy, all that sugar, but I figure we're on vacation, right?"

"Right," Joey said.

They drove on due south through Cheyenne and the flat brown high prairie that stretched from Canada south to New Mexico on the eastern side of the Rockies. By two-thirty they were in the northern suburbs of Denver.

Callie had already figured out the best route to Mase's house, but Joey had assured her his dad had showed him the way, so she pretended to consult him now. "Okay," Callie said, dodging city traffic on the eight-lane interstate, "can you get me to your house?"

"Um, sure. Just get off on University, then I'll show you."

"You want to call your dad? He's probably at work, but we could try to reach him there."

"No," Joey said, "please, Callie, please. I want to surprise him."

"Some people don't like surprises a whole lot, pard-ner."

"He will, I know he will."

Joey directed her quite handily down University Avenue, past the undergrad hangouts of D.U. students, around a corner, past a small park and onto a quiet street lined with older brick houses and tall trees. Kids were riding their tricycles on the sidewalk while dogs dozed on front stoops.

Callie drove slowly, curious as the devil. So this was where Mase lived, where he and his wife, Amy, had lived, where Joey had probably been born.

"There!" Joey cried, pointing. "There it is!"

He indicated a neat brick house with white shutters,

a brick sidewalk leading up to the door, some juniper shrubs and a manicured front lawn. No flowers, though. No lady to plant flowers.

"Turn in the driveway, right there," Joey was saying, almost beside himself with eagerness.

She pulled in and parked, then got out of the truck and stretched. Joey scrambled across the seat to her side and jumped down. "Come on, I know where the key is," he said. "In back, come on." He took her hand and tugged on it.

"Hey, okay, I'm coming," Callie said, laughing.

Her laugh would have shut off like a spigot if she had noticed the black station wagon parked across the street. Her blood would have curdled in her veins had she seen the man sitting inside behind the tinted windows, intently watching Mase's house. The trepidation and anticipation of seeing Mase would have been dashed instantly if she'd noted that the cadaverous-faced man in the car suddenly grinned. Wickedly.

Finding the key under the doormat—"Original," Callie muttered—Joey opened the back door.

Callie couldn't help herself. She walked through the kitchen noting everything—colors, cabinets, dishes in the sink, chairs, living room furniture, a newspaper thrown carelessly on the green velour couch. The bookshelves, the television set, the closed drapes.

The house was neat but dusty. It had been decorated by a woman, but not kept up by one.

"Come see my room," Joey was saying. "Callie, please."

She followed the little boy, her fingers trailing across a tabletop. She stopped for a moment to study a grouping of carefully framed photographs of the LeBow family. Baby pictures of Joey, a photo of Mase, a younger

Mase, proud and smiling in a police uniform. Some momentous occasion, she supposed. Graduation from the police academy?

Wedding pictures.

"Callie! Come on!" Joey piped up.

"Just a minute," Callie said, but it was more to herself than Joey. The pictures. A young and handsome Mase in a tuxedo posing next to his wife. Amy. Amy LeBow. Mrs. Amy LeBow. Awfully pretty. Dark hair pulled back beneath her wedding veil. A pixie face. Almond-shaped eyes, high cheekbones, a wide, smiling mouth. Joey had her eyes and tawny coloring.

"Callie!"

"Okay, I'm coming." She went down the hall, past a bathroom cluttered with male paraphernalia and a bedroom with a hastily made bed. Next to the bedroom was an office with papers piled on a desk, and then Joey's room.

Red-and-blue quilts with sports figures on them draped the deep blue walls, and balsa-wood airplanes hung from the ceiling. There was a set of wooden bunk beds, and fluffy white clouds were painted on the ceiling. Dinosaur figurines covered the desk and dresser, vicious, growling creatures to delight a boy's heart. Someone had lovingly planned this room for a cherished child. Who else but Joey's mother?

"See?" Joey said. "I told you."

"It's...well, it's wonderful, kiddo. Absolutely fantastic."

"I know." He looked very serious. "My grandma and grandpa told me it was the best room ever."

"It is."

"And my other grandma and grandpa, from New

Mexico—'' he pointed up ''—they said my mommy painted those clouds for me.''

"Oh, Joey," Callie began.

"She painted good, huh?"

"Oh, yes, your mother painted the most beautiful clouds ever."

"I know," he said again, so proud.

Back in the living room, Callie asked Joey what they should do. "Should we just wait? Or call your grandparents or your dad's office?"

"We can wait here."

"Hmm, we're going to get hungry eventually. Do you suppose there's anything in the fridge?"

"Daddy hates grocery shopping."

"Me, too." She put her hands on her hips. "Think he'd mind if I looked around in there?"

"Nah, he doesn't care."

"What're you going to do, pardner?"

"Watch TV." Joey found the remote, settled in what was obviously his favorite chair and began to click away happily.

The fridge was all but empty. There was some butter, old yogurt, a six-pack of beer, a package of withered carrots and some moldy bagels.

"Ye gods," Callie muttered. "No wonder he liked Francine's food."

"Pizza," Joey said, appearing in the kitchen doorway.

"Is that what your dad does?" Callie asked. "Order out for pizza?"

Joey lifted his shoulders. "Uh-huh, lots of times."

"I can see why."

"I like sausage," he said matter-of-factly. "The phone number's there."

"Okay, sounds like a good idea."

They'd finished the pizza and soft drinks and were watching TV together when Joey looked up, listened for a minute, then said, "Daddy's home."

Callie jerked upright. "How do you know?"

"I heard his car."

"Oh." She ran a hand through her hair and tucked her blouse in. She barely had time to take a calming breath when Mase burst in through the front door.

He stood there, his face black with rage, his body taut as a bowstring. He was wearing a dark suit with shirt and tie, loosened at the collar, and there was a suspicious bulge at his hip. Homicide Detective Mason LeBow.

"What in hell are you doing here?" he rasped.

"Hi, Daddy," Joey said, running to him. "Surprise!"

"*Surprise,*" Mase repeated, chewing on the word. "Whose idea was this surprise?"

"Mine, Daddy. I wanted to show Callie my room and…"

"Joey, maybe you better let me talk to your dad for a minute," Callie said, her gaze holding Mase's. "Can we go into the kitchen?"

She was almost afraid to turn her back on him, but she did. She walked ahead of him into the kitchen and he followed.

"Okay," he said, his voice low and harsh, "what's going on here?"

"How's your head?" she asked in a classic non sequitur.

"My head?"

"The cut."

He put a hand up to the Band-Aid on his forehead.

"It's fine," he said impatiently. "Now, answer me, Callie. What are you doing here?"

"Joey was homesick," she said, trying to keep her voice steady. She'd thought he might be a little irritated, but his reaction was so extreme it scared her. "We all thought it would be good for him to be home for a few days. He's only six."

"Oh, God." Mase ran a hand through his dark hair. "Homesick."

"Yes. He did great for the first few days, then he got a little upset. And seeing as he's been so...well, sensitive, we all thought..."

Mase held a hand up. "I understand. I'm sorry. It was just such a shock to see you both here."

"I wanted to call, but Joey insisted on surprising you."

"Oh, God," Mase said again.

"Is something wrong?" Callie asked, her brow knitting suspiciously.

He shook his head. "Nothing, no. It was a shock, that's all." He frowned and looked at her. "Why you?"

"Why me what?"

"Why did you drive him here?"

She could feel two fiery splotches on her cheeks. "I, um, well, they all made me come. I, well, they said I should go shopping."

Mase turned away and massaged the back of his neck with a hand. He muttered something she couldn't hear. Then he turned around and said, "You and Joey have to leave. Tomorrow, first thing. Go back to the ranch."

"Excuse me?"

"You can't stay here."

"Well, I wasn't planning to, for your information."
Callie drew herself up. "I delivered Joey, and now I'll
leave and find myself a nice motel, and tomorrow I'll
go…"

"The hell you will."

"The hell I will *what?*"

"Get a motel. You'll stay here tonight, and you'll
take Joey and…"

"I'll do whatever I darn well please, Mr. LeBow,"
Callie shot back.

"Damn it, Callie, you'll do what I want you to do
with my son."

"What is he, a puppy? And who do you think you
are to order—"

"No, no, I mean…"

"I know what you mean," she said testily. "You've
probably got some hot date lined up for the weekend,
and you're furious we showed up."

Mase was silent for a long time. Callie crossed her
arms over her chest and glared at him.

"Is that what you think?" he finally asked.

"Yes, that's what I think. Why should I think dif-
ferently? You haven't even said hello to your own
son."

Mase rubbed his hand over his face. "Damn…"

"Okay, I know when I'm not wanted. I'll leave
now," she said, "but it sure would be nice if you gave
Joey a big hug." She felt hurt and humiliated. Some
surprise this had been.

"Okay," Mase said, "let's start over. I'm sorry I
yelled. I do *not* have a hot date. I'm very glad to see
Joey." He swallowed. "And you. Please stay here.
There's a guest room."

It occurred to Callie that it cost Mase an awful lot

to say that. Fleetingly, she wondered why he'd bothered, but the anger and the pain she felt overrode any questions.

"Daddy?"

They both turned their heads as if a puppeteer had pulled their strings. Joey was standing in the kitchen doorway. "Daddy, are you mad?"

Mase took a deep breath. "No, Joey, I was just surprised." He went to his son, reached down and hugged him. "It's great to see you."

"Callie wants to go shopping," Joey said.

Mase looked at her. "I'm afraid there won't be time for shopping. She's going to have to take you back to the ranch tomorrow."

"Excuse me, Mase," Callie said, trying to keep her voice under control, "but I'm not leaving Denver till I'm good and ready. I didn't drive this far to turn around and go home. Now, either you tell me why we have to go back to Wyoming, whatever crazy reason you have, or I'm going to find a motel right next door to the Cherry Creek Mall, and I'm going shopping."

"You're not going to a motel," he said between clenched teeth. "I told you, you can stay here."

"Callie, don't go," Joey cried.

"You don't want me here," Callie said.

"Yes we do," Joey replied. "Don't we, Daddy?"

"Yes," Mase agreed. Reluctantly.

All of a sudden she felt weary, tired from driving, from the anticipation and disappointment, from everything. She was too exhausted to drive through the city and look for a motel, and she didn't want to stay all by herself. "Okay, I'll stay here," she agreed, "but I'm going shopping tomorrow. You don't have to come, and I can take Joey and…"

"I wouldn't miss your shopping trip for the world," Mase said, interrupting her. "We'll all go."

Callie finally settled down in the guest room, after Mase had taken some boxes and piles of papers off the bed. They'd both tucked Joey in, very uncomfortable with each other, and Callie had retired to her room as soon as she could, but not before Mase had tried to apologize again.

"Look, I didn't expect you," he said. "I had a hard day."

"You know, Mase," she said tiredly, "somehow I think it's a whole lot more than that."

"No, it isn't. What do you think it is? God, Callie, I drove home from work, and there's your truck in the driveway, and I thought something had happened to Joey."

"Yeah, sure. Well, Mase, it doesn't matter. We're here. I should have called first, I know that now, okay?"

After he left, she lay in bed, trying to sleep, her body thrumming with tension. She could hear Mase moving around, could hear the water gurgling in the pipes as he used the bathroom. Then his footsteps went past her door to the living room, and she heard the low murmur of the TV. What did Mase sleep in? Did he have pajamas on? Or just his underwear? Without a bridging thought, she saw him in boxer shorts and a T-shirt. She'd never seen his legs, but they were muscular in her imagination, covered with curling hairs. His feet... She wondered what his feet were like. Long and well shaped...?

What would happen if she got up, walked down the hall to the living room and asked him point-blank what was wrong? Why had he been so upset at their arrival?

What secret problem did he have? She lay there in the
guest room and knew she wouldn't do it. She was
afraid to. Callie Thorne, who was never afraid to face
difficult situations, was scared.

CHAPTER NINE

MASE HADN'T SLEPT MUCH, and he was tired and cranky. He'd tossed and turned all night, knowing Callie was just across the hall. He wondered if Callie slept on her side or on her back. He saw her fine golden hair spread on the pillow, her thin arms hugging it, her legs tangled in the sheet. He dozed and jerked awake a hundred times, and he swore to himself in the darkness, positive he could hear her breathing.

He got up early, made coffee and padded around silently, trying not to make any noise. He picked up the paper from his front steps, looking up and down the street for suspicious vehicles or people. Crazy, paranoid.

There was no way to get Callie and Joey out of Denver quickly without telling her the truth, and he still couldn't do that. Maybe someday, after the trial, he could explain, but not now. Part of him wanted to tell her. Another part, the cop part, knew he had to keep his cards close to his chest.

He pulled on jeans and a T-shirt and sat at the table drinking coffee and reading the paper. He was troubled. Had he put Callie in danger by leaving Joey with her? It was bad enough that Metcalf had threatened Joey, but to drag in an innocent stranger was inexcusable.

Callie got up at eight and came into the kitchen in jeans and a sweatshirt. She was sleepy-eyed, her hair pulled back with a clip, wisps falling over her cheeks. He looked down at the paper, rattling it, and tried to ignore her presence. It was no use. It had been too long since he'd been in a situation like this with a woman. An eternity, it seemed right now. And, damn it, she looked downright adorable.

"Is Joey up yet?" she asked, helping herself to coffee.

"Not yet." He rattled the paper again.

"Mmm." She stretched, yawning. "I actually slept in. What a treat."

Mase almost said something about his night, but he held his tongue. "So, what're your plans?"

"Plans? I have no plans. The mall later. Say, do you have anything for breakfast around here? I got us pizza for dinner because there wasn't much in the fridge."

"Yeah, sorry. I've been working a lot, eating out. I didn't expect houseguests."

"Right."

He finally rose, rummaged around in a cupboard and pulled out a box of toaster pastries.

"Ugh." Callie made a face.

"This seems to be it."

"Okay, they'll do. I'm starved."

"I'll go grocery shopping later," Mase promised. "I'll even cook dinner, my special spaghetti and clam sauce."

"Sure, fine. I thought we'd go out, though."

"Afraid to try my cooking?"

She cocked her head and looked at him. "No. Let's just say I'll reserve judgment."

Mase went back to the paper while Callie toasted her pastries—three of them. While she waited, she leaned on the counter, drumming her fingers and gazing idly out the window. He couldn't help glancing from time to time at her jeans-clad derriere, the slim, firm roundness. He felt annoyed, curiously and irrationally bothered by her presence. He'd been doing just fine without a female in the house. It had been hard—harder than he could have imagined—adjusting to the loss of Amy, but he had survived. He hadn't thought much about his own needs in the past year. But now... Well, damn, it was impossible not to acknowledge one particular need. His brain shied away from it, but his body was betraying him.

Go home, Callie Thorne.

IT WAS ALMOST LUNCHTIME when they were finally organized and on their way to the Cherry Creek Mall.

It was crowded with weekend shoppers, and Joey headed straight for the newly installed play area, where he crawled and slid and jumped with the other kids.

Callie sat with Mase for a while, watching Joey, along with the other mothers and fathers and grandparents, but Mase could tell she was antsy.

"Why don't you go shopping?" he asked. "We'll wait here."

"Don't you want to go, too?"

"Shopping? But I don't need anything."

She cocked her head. "What does that have to do with it?"

He looked at her. "That's a joke, right?"

She smiled. "Sort of. Maybe. Not really."

"Go on," he said. "There's Saks and Neiman Marcus and Anne Klein over there."

"Anne Klein," Callie said, laughing. "On the ranch?"

"We'll be okay here," Mase insisted. He needed a

breather from Callie, neutral ground where he could get back some kind of control.

She finally went off on her own, and Mase took a deep breath. He sat there and watched his son play and pretended that this Saturday was just an ordinary day.

Mase had never been a good shopper. Malls and department stores made him nervous. Some guys, he realized, were great at it. Tolerant, patient, they happily hung out in bookstores or sport shops while their mates perused every item, every sale rack. But not him. And today was worse. He knew he was being paranoid, but he couldn't help studying faces, looking for one in particular—Hank Berry's. The idea that the Hitman would actually shadow them in a mall was nuts. Still, Mase scanned the weekend crowds, his heart beating just a little bit erratically.

Callie returned after an hour or so, and Joey teased her about all the bags she was carrying.

"What did you get?" he asked. "What did you get, Callie?"

"Oh, some stuff," she said. "Nothing you'd be interested in."

"Did you get Rebecca anything?" Joey asked suddenly.

"Well, I..."

"Let's get her something, okay?"

"Sure," Callie said, "but you have to pick it out."

It took Joey a long time to decide what to buy for his new friend. He started in the toy store with stuffed animals, but quickly discarded each one.

"Nah. She won't like this," he said about a stuffed green dinosaur. "Girls don't like dinosaurs much."

He checked out the entire store, from toy soldiers to trains to models to building blocks to talking dolls to

Beanie Babies. And, thank heavens, he stopped with the bean-bag animals.

"What do you think, Callie?" he asked, holding out a yellow duck with a bright orange beak. "I think Rebecca would like this one."

"Oh, absolutely," Callie concurred.

"That's definitely the one," Mase said, breathing a visible sigh of relief.

Mase paid at the counter while Joey did another turn in the aisles and Callie waited by the door.

"I'm hungry," Joey said, when he and Mase rejoined her.

"Lunch, then," Callie began, then she looked at Mase. "That okay with you?"

"Sure, lunch," he said, and he followed behind while Joey hung on Callie's hand and skipped along beside her.

They got a table in a Mexican restaurant, a popular spot in the mall. Callie said, "I'm starved," in that lilting voice of hers, as if she were surprised by the fact that she was hungry, as if it were a wondrous new sensation. She ordered a taco plate, her appetite healthy as usual. She was smiling, carefree, chatting with Joey, oblivious to any possible danger. As she should be. She looked awfully pretty, in a blue denim skirt and a round-necked pink T-shirt that showed her delicate collarbone. And pink lipstick. Her hair was pulled up on top of her head and fastened there in some mysterious way that eluded Mase, and wisps curled down around her neck. He couldn't keep his eyes off her ears and her neck and the hollow at the base of her throat that Ralph Fiennes had made such a goddamn fuss over in that movie they'd seen.

After lunch they strolled together through the mall.

He bought Joey a handheld computer game in one store, and Joey played it the rest of the time, bumping into people, so rapt was he.

Victoria's Secret did Mase in.

"Do you mind if I run in here for a sec?" Callie asked.

He waited for her in the front of the shop, Joey beside him, still immersed in his game. Mase felt entirely out of place, embarrassed to death as his eyes roamed over the racks of silky negligees, bras and panties and the shelves of colorful, exotic fragrances.

There were two men in the shop helping their ladyfriends select underwear—*helping*. Mase was utterly bewildered. He could never, ever pick out a woman's underthingies. He'd rather die first. He guessed that made him some sort of a Neanderthal, certainly no Renaissance man. Well, so be it. He'd rather crouch over a fire in a cave making grunting noises than pick up the white lacy thing on that shelf and say, "Here, honey, these are *you*." No bloody way.

He was immensely relieved when he saw Callie paying for something at the cash register. Something filmy and black that the girl behind the counter was folding carefully.

"Thanks," Callie said as she came up to him. "I saw that in their catalog and I just had to get it."

Mase said nothing.

They took Joey into a nature store, but he was really more interested in his game. Callie bought some novelty items for her mother and her sister-in-law. "Oh, they'll love these," she declared triumphantly.

"Very nice," Mase said.

"Hey, would it be too much to ask to go to the Tattered Cover? It's right across the street, and I'm hoping they'll have a book I've been trying to find. About equine therapy."

"Sure, why not? I'll get something for Joey. They have a wonderful children's section." The bookstore was much more to his liking than women's lingerie. Nice and neutral.

The famous Denver gathering place was jammed. They split up, and Callie promised to find them in the children's section.

Joey picked out a beautifully illustrated book about, of all things, horses.

"This is the one you want, you're sure?" Mase asked.

"Yes, I do. I really do. I'll ask Callie to read it to me."

Callie. Callie and her horses.

She arrived in a few minutes, pushing her way through the crowd, breathless.

"I got it," she declared. "Can you believe they actually had it?"

"Look at my new book," Joey said, pulling it out of the bag.

"Oh, how wonderful," she said. "I'll read it to you tonight, okay?"

"Okay."

Mase scowled. She could read his own kid's mind. What was she, some kind of witch?

But, Mase had to admit, Joey was a different child now. She'd done that—or her ranch had. No longer was his son afraid and clinging. He was a normal little boy again. Giggling, playing his video game, enthusiastic. And he was obviously very close to Callie. Very, very close.

What in hell would happen when the trial was over

and Joey came home again? He'd lost his mother a year ago. Was he to lose another woman he loved? Abruptly Mase felt a cold hand on the back of his neck. Had he made a terrible mistake leaving Joey at the Someday Ranch? It had been convenient. Had he taken the path of least resistance without regard to the future?

After the Tattered Cover, the three of them strolled through the outside shopping area behind the Cherry Creek Mall.

"I'm starving," Callie said, stopping in front of the frozen yogurt shop.

Mase stared at her and shook his head. "Starved. Of course you are," he said just loud enough for her to hear.

But she didn't seem to mind. She only shrugged, and he detected a little twinkle in her eyes.

They sat on the benches in front of the shop, frozen yogurt melting in the hot sun. Joey soon had chocolate all over his face, between his fingers, down the front of his shirt. Callie got a cup of water from the shop and cleaned him off with wet napkins.

"There," she said. "Presentable."

On the way home Mase pulled into the parking lot of a supermarket.

"You want to wait here?" he asked.

"Heck, no. It's air-conditioned inside. Come on, pardner," she said to Joey.

The cart filled up quickly. Callie roved up and down the aisles, reappearing with various items she said Mase absolutely needed: ice cream, chocolate sauce, pretzels, cookies, bags of ready-made salad, Caesar dressing, a string of garlic.

"We can't eat all of that. When you're gone it'll spoil."

"The only thing that'll spoil is the salad. And you should eat a lot of that, because it's healthy."

"And the rest of this stuff is healthy?"

"I believe in a balanced diet," Callie said loftily.

Mase made dinner that night. He didn't tell Callie that spaghetti was the only thing he knew how to cook. She leaned on a counter, legs crossed at the ankles in front of her, and watched.

"Men look so funny in the kitchen," she said.

"Oh, you mean all those great international chefs look funny?" he asked, chopping scallions.

"No, I mean regular men. Like you and my dad."

He heated up a skillet and poured in some olive oil.

"Mmm, smells good."

"Nothing's cooking yet."

"I like the smell of hot olive oil."

He sautéed the scallions, lots of them.

"Now it really smells good," she said.

"What time are you going to leave tomorrow?" Mase asked.

"Oh, I don't know. Whenever. Why, you dying to get rid of us?"

"No, I was thinking of breakfast and lunch."

"There's plenty of food."

He had his head down, concentrating hard on the sizzling scallions. "Look," he finally said, "I just want you to know I appreciate what you've done for Joey. He's changed a lot."

"Oh," Callie said, flushing, "it's nothing. I didn't do anything. Big deal, so I put him on a gentle old mare."

"You did more than that," Mase said. "You loved him. Everyone on your ranch loved him."

"He's not hard to love, Mase."

"But he's not your son. You didn't have to—"

"Stop. You don't have to thank me. It's what I do. I see someone, anyone—big, small, old, young—who needs help, and I do what I can."

"That magic again, huh?"

"Yes, that's part of it. The rest is just old-fashioned caring."

They pried Joey away from his game and ate dinner, then Callie fixed them banana splits. Joey tried his best to finish, but the ice cream melted, and he promptly fell asleep on the couch.

"Should we put him to bed?" Callie asked.

"Later," Mase replied, so they did the dishes and cleaned up the kitchen. Like some old married couple.

Well, it *was* nice to have a female in the house. If his mother could see him now, she'd be setting the wedding date. She badly wanted Mase to remarry. "Get a mother for that child," she'd been saying lately. And his mother would like Callie a lot; they'd get on like a house afire.

Which was why, Mase thought, he hadn't called his folks. They'd make such a damn fuss.

Mase woke Joey up and got him to bed.

"Where's Callie?" the boy asked sleepily. "I want her to read the book to me."

"It's too late tonight. How about you take the book back to the ranch with you? She'll have more time to read it there."

"Okay. Can I say good-night to her, Daddy?"

"Sure."

So Callie came into Joey's blue bedroom and sat on the edge of his bed, smoothed the hair off his forehead and whispered good-night. *Just like Amy used to*, Mase thought, his throat tightening.

Callie wanted to watch her favorite program on television, *Early Edition*. Mase had never heard of it, but it was about a guy who routinely foresaw dire newspaper headlines before the events took place, then he had to go out and remedy the disaster that was going to happen. There was also a magic cat in the program. Of course.

"Whoever thought of that idea?" Callie asked when it was over. "How can people be so clever?"

"Because they're paid. It's their job," Mase replied dryly.

"Oh, you're such a cynic."

He grunted something noncommittal.

For a time, Callie channel-surfed, delighting in all the shows Mase got on his cable TV system. "Gosh," she said, "I wish Dad would get a satellite. We don't have cable, you know, out in the sticks."

"There are worse things," Mase said, and he couldn't help eyeing the way she unconsciously curled and uncurled her toes as she sat, bare feet up on the couch. Pretty toes. Pretty feet. Pretty ankles and calves and nicely shaped knees. Smooth, slightly tanned skin, silky looking. He couldn't stop himself from wondering how that skin would feel against his.

Stop it, he told himself angrily, but again his body refused to cooperate. It was suddenly way too hot inside, and he rose and went to the back screen door, opening it and breathing in the cooler night air.

Please, Callie, go home.

When he finally walked back into the living room, the nightly news was on.

Callie looked up and pointed to the screen, where an anchorwoman was giving a summary of the day's news events in the Denver area. "I could do that," Callie declared.

He sat, knees splayed, and said, "What?"

"I could be a newsperson. Well," she clarified, "I mean, I once did this spot on the Casper news, for the therapy ranch, you know, and I did okay. Everyone who watched it said I looked relaxed and all. I was nervous when I was actually doing the taping, but when I saw it, I wasn't bad at all. It was fun." That telltale color rose in her cheeks then. "Oh, listen to me bragging. I'd probably be horrible at it. Really. And if I did that, who would do the therapy?"

The question came out before Mase even realized he'd thought it. "Don't you ever want to marry and have a family?" he asked, and then he could have kicked himself. She'd take it all wrong.

"Oh," she said, waving a hand, "of course I'd like all the normal things. You know. But nothing will stop me from helping people. And why should it, anyway?"

"No reason," Mase said.

"Did Amy work?" she asked abruptly.

"Up until Joey was born she did. She planned to go back to work after he started first grade. But..." He shrugged.

"I guess I'm lucky," Callie said. "I don't have to stop work ever. Well, if I ever have a baby, maybe for a few months, I suppose. But I figure I'll always be around the ranch, and with Mom and Dad right there... Yes, I am lucky." She turned away then and went back to the news, looking ill at ease. He felt the same. He hadn't meant to get into such a personal conversation.

He didn't have any interest in her future plans. She was a cowgirl, a rancher, an equine therapist, and he was a cop, a city boy. Two different worlds. And that was fine by him.

When the news was over, she got up and stretched. "I think I'm tired from shopping. Malls do me in. If you don't mind, I'll turn in."

He nodded, studying her.

"Well, good night, Mase," she said.

"Good night," he said, and he watched her disappear down the hall.

He was exhausted, but he slept fitfully, one ear open as usual for strange noises outside the house. When he was awake, he thought about the events of the day and how happy Joey seemed. He sent a thought up to Amy: *I'm doing my best, honey. Joey's fine. He's going to be okay.*

Mase thought about the day he'd spent with Callie, and he couldn't help remembering that store she'd gone into. All that lace and silk, the whisper-thin straps and flowing satiny gowns. And Callie's purchase, a little scrap of black.

Was she wearing it now? Did she have her new nightie on right now? He couldn't help seeing her in it, the black against her creamy skin. The straps resting lightly on her smooth shoulders, the hem caressing her thighs. Oh, Lord.

Eventually he dozed. He was awakened sometime later, in the pitch-black, by noises in the kitchen, stealthy noises that made him sit bolt upright. Wide-awake, he reached for his service revolver in the night-table drawer.

His heart pounded in adrenaline-powered bursts as

he moved silently out of his bedroom and down the hall. It was dark, but he knew the house while the intruder didn't. He'd edged past Callie's door, sliding along the wall in the shadows. He heard a small noise again, a cupboard door opening, and moved faster, through the living room to the kitchen. His eyes were growing accustomed to the dark, and he made out a shadow that detached itself from the blackness. *Gotcha*, he thought, reaching out one hand to the light switch and clicking the safety off his revolver with the other.

Mase blinked once in the blinding light, heard a muffled scream and assumed the shooter's stance.

It was Callie.

"Oh, my God," she gasped, one hand to her throat, eyes wide.

Mase stared at her and swore. He lowered the gun and sagged against the wall. "Goddamn it, Callie," he breathed. "I could have shot you."

"I...I...there was no glass in the bathroom so I..." she babbled. "A drink, a drink of water, so I..."

"I thought someone broke in," he said raggedly.

"Oh, God, I...I'm sorry."

She *was* wearing the Victoria's Secret nightie, a short black thing, a scrap of lace leaving her shoulders bare—and her arms and her legs. His eyes feasted on the sight for a heartbeat in time, then he switched his gaze to her face.

"I'm sorry, too," he said. "I must have scared you to death."

She gave a shaky laugh. "That's a big gun you've got there."

"What? Oh." He looked down at his service revolver, hastily switched the safety on and laid it on the kitchen table.

Callie was hugging herself, standing there barefoot in the middle of his kitchen. And, Mase realized suddenly, all he wore was pajama bottoms.

"I...I guess I should have gotten a glass of water before I went to bed," she whispered.

"No, no, it's my fault. I shouldn't have..."

"I'm so embarrassed."

They stood there, silent for a long moment, too silent, eyes locked. Both of them had far too much bare skin showing, and Mase felt a slow heat build in his belly.

Callie drew in a quavering breath and tried to smile. "I guess...I better let you get back to bed."

"Yeah." But he didn't move.

Callie moved, though, toward him, still hugging herself, and he had to step back to let her pass. He caught a whiff of her scent, shampoo and a faint aroma of vanilla. He could hear the silky swish of the black negligee against her skin. His belly tightened.

"Uh...sorry about this," she said in a small voice.

"Yeah." He rubbed a hand across his face.

"Good night," she whispered, slipping past him and going down the dark hall, disappearing into her bedroom.

He must have been holding his breath all this time, because suddenly his lungs were starved for oxygen. He drew air in deeply, shook his head. He could have shot Callie. He could have...

He could have taken her into his arms and kissed her, he thought, then blocked out the notion instantly.

He checked the locks on the doors and windows,

then picked up his pistol from the table. Once he had turned the light off, he padded down the hall to his room. The house was cool, but Mase lay in bed sweating.

He couldn't wait till Callie went back to Wyoming. Then maybe he'd get some goddamn sleep.

OUTSIDE MASE LEBOW'S HOUSE, the Hitman crossed the street. He'd been about to do the job a few minutes ago when the lights suddenly came on in the place, and he'd stopped, frozen. Now everything was dark and silent again, and he could do what he'd come for and get out of there.

Somewhere a dog barked, and he halted, listening. He hated dogs. But this one was far away and quiet now, so he continued on. He reached the driveway and switched on the high-tech, focused-beam flashlight. Taking the tracking device out of the pocket of his trench coat, he knelt down next to the woman's muddy pickup.

He made a face as he stuck the device onto the bottom of the truck. It was filthy and probably had horse manure all over it. Distasteful. Hank was used to freshly detailed BMWs in spotless garages.

But he knew it was vital he keep track of the cop's kid. Hank had discussed the whole thing with Metcalf at length—LeBow wouldn't open his mouth at the trial if there was a threat to his kid. No testimony, no case.

Besides, Metcalf wouldn't pay Hank the hundred thousand he owed him if the cop testified.

It had been touch-and-go there for a while when LeBow's kid had disappeared last week. Hank had been nervous, but he'd also been patient, and it had paid off. Lo and behold, the kid had reappeared, and with a pretty young chick, too. Hank wasn't going to lose him again.

He checked the tracking device to make sure it was fastened firmly on the underside of the pickup, then slowly straightened, dusting his hands off. As he slinked back into the shadows, he was smiling to himself. *Got you, LeBow.*

CHAPTER TEN

JOEY SLEPT ON THE SEAT next to Callie almost the whole way back to the ranch. Only once did they stop, at a roadside rest station, and he'd gone to the bathroom and bought a bag of chips from a vending machine. He hadn't even finished the chips when he nodded off again.

Kids aren't so hard to raise, Callie thought, smiling as she drove. Mase's kid, anyway.

She chewed the notion over the whole way. Mase's child. His *motherless* child. She tried not to dwell on it, but it was so difficult. And last night. The way Mase had looked at her. His bare chest with its triangle of dark hair, his muscular arms, his strong neck. He'd scared her to death. Her heart had nearly burst through her chest, but it hadn't all been fear. No, some of it had been plain old desire. And Mase, he'd felt something, too. She knew he had.

She almost groaned out loud as she drove through Cheyenne. Why had she worn the new nightgown to bed? Had some perverse, mischief-making imp taken hold of her? Why not her usual extra-large T-shirt?

She couldn't stop thinking about him, about his child. About crazy, impossible dreams. And she couldn't wipe the secret smile from her lips. Nothing could wipe it away, not even the knowledge that Mase was keeping something from her, something awfully important. All she had to do was picture him, and her heart kicked at her ribs.

Reality intruded the minute she got out of the truck with Joey and her shopping bags when Sylvia hurried up to them.

"Oh, my gosh," she said, wringing her hands. "I'm so glad you're back. And Joey... Oh, my."

It wasn't long before Callie had the story. Not an hour after they'd left for Denver, Rebecca had disappeared. They'd found her within minutes, luckily, hiding under her bed in the bunkhouse. But she'd been despondent ever since, not eating, just sitting near Francine, silent and unreachable.

Callie looked down at Joey and frowned. My Lord, she thought, what was going to happen to Rebecca when Joey left for good?

As Callie suspected, Rebecca came around the minute Joey ran into the kitchen, bubbling over with all his news. He told her that he got to show Callie his house and dinosaurs and everything. And his new video game. Then he handed her the Beanie Baby. Callie, Sylvia, Francine and Liz stood there and watched a tiny smile touch Rebecca's lips as she clutched the yellow duck. Two hours later, Rebecca had eaten her first real meal in days and was climbing the fence surrounding the riding ring with Joey and Peter, her new toy still in hand.

Even Tom Thorne saw the astounding response in the child. "I don't know what she's going to do when Mase picks up Joey for good," Callie's dad said solemnly.

Everyone agreed. They all remarked on Joey and Rebecca's strange bond. And they all looked to Callie for an answer. As if she had one.

The call came from Mase shortly before dinner. "It's for you, honey," Callie's mom said, handing her the portable phone and winking conspiratorially.

Callie took the phone and climbed the stairs to her private spot. As she sat, sighing to herself, she realized everyone at the ranch was pairing her up with Mase—even her folks. If they only knew...

"Hello," she said, keeping her tone neutral.

And the first words out of his mouth were "You got there okay? You're safe?"

"Of course we did," she said. "We got home just fine. Is there some reason we shouldn't have?"

Mase said something about the weekend traffic on I-25 and the thirty-mile construction zone and a storm—though Callie hadn't seen a cloud in the sky. She listened to his voice, to the deep male timbre of his voice, and closed her eyes, letting herself pretend he was sitting there next to her. Yet all the time she knew there was something wrong, something Mase was keeping from her.

They talked for a few minutes, and Callie related the story of Rebecca's response to Joey's return. She couldn't say the obvious, that the little girl was going to fall back into that dark hole when Joey left for good. But Mase knew what she was getting at.

"It's quite a strange relationship," he said. "Who would have dreamed it?"

I would have, Callie thought, but she kept her musings to herself. Instead, she said, "Is everything okay there?"

"Sure," he said, "of course."

"You have to work tomorrow?"

"Every Monday, sure."

"And there's no problem at work?"

"No, of course not," he said. "Listen, I better go. I just wanted to make sure you got home without any trouble."

Callie let out a breath. "Okay," she said, "well, goodbye."

"I'll call. In a couple days, all right?"

"That would be fine."

"Give Joey a hug for me?"

"I will," she said.

She'd tried to keep her voice even, tried not to pry too hard into his life. But, darn it, he was being deceitful. She knew it. And it wasn't fair. She rose and went down to dinner, putting on a cheerful face. But, oh, how hard it was. She hurt inside. Every time she thought about Mase or glanced at Joey, she ached. She desperately wanted Mase to trust her. She *needed* him to trust her.

MASE GOT INTO THE SHOWER on Monday morning, his head still full of images of Callie and Joey here in this house. A house that had seemed too damn empty since Amy's death.

He lathered his chest and remembered Joey yesterday, jumping with excitement at the prospect of leaving for Wyoming. The boy had babbled about Francine and her chocolate cake and his new friends, Rebecca and Peter. In fact, he'd been bubbling with anticipation. It was difficult, but Mase was beginning to douse that ember of resentment he'd first felt. Joey truly was coming out of the depression he'd been in this last year. It was as if a weight had been lifted from Mase's shoulders, one he hadn't acknowledged was even there. Was it the ranch or Callie that had made the difference? Callie with her terminal optimism.

Curiously, it had been both difficult and easy to ask Callie if Joey could stay on at the Someday Ranch for a couple more weeks. Easy for Joey's sake. But real hard for Mase. Not because he felt beholden to her. And not even because he was worried sick about his son's safety. It had been difficult because he was lying to Callie Thorne. Lying to the most unselfish, honest person he'd ever met.

He got out of the shower and cleared a spot in the foggy mirror, meeting his own eyes. Damn, but he hated deceiving her. He'd never thought it was going to happen again, never thought a woman rambling around his house could feel so right. Yet, amazingly, Callie's presence here had brought him such pleasure he was stunned. He'd never met anyone like her— never knew people like Callie existed. And he wasn't being honest with her.

He tugged on his trousers and zipped them up, staring at the unmade bed. Despite himself, despite the hopelessness of the situation, he stared long and hard at the bed, seeing Callie there in her new nightgown, the smooth material lying against her skin, every curve and hollow and lean line revealed in stark relief. He saw her as clearly as if she were really there, the small firm breasts, the shadow of her womanhood, the pale fine flesh of her arms and thighs.

He ached fiercely but couldn't stop staring and fantasizing. Sure, okay, he was a man, and it had been a long time, but this was more. He craved her, the silkiness of her breasts against him, the scent of her. He craved her very soul. He stared at the bed he'd shared with his wife, and he felt the throb of life in his veins again, the need, the longing, the sweet pain of desire for another person.

Mase finally tore his gaze from the sheets and pulled on a shirt. He threw his suit jacket on and stuffed a tie in the pocket. Although he tried not to look at the bed again, her face stayed in his head—the whimsical expressions, the spots of red rising on her cheeks, the dancing light in her hazel eyes.

Yesterday, when she and Joey had driven off, Mase had gotten in his car and secretly followed them for the first fifty miles to make damn good and sure he was the only one on their tail. He remembered his relief that they were okay—and a curious regret that he wasn't going back to the ranch with them.

Mase grabbed an apple and headed out to his car, trying to get Callie and Joey out of his thoughts. He needed to concentrate on the trial and on Hank Berry, who, he was positive, was close by. He didn't have time to dwell on Callie.

And yet it was impossible to let go of her. Magic, she'd told him, the ranch was magic. But she was dead wrong. It was Callie who was magic.

Mase parked in his usual spot in the lot across from the downtown Denver police headquarters. He strode past the row of bail bondsmen offices located in brightly painted Victorian houses and locked his jaw— same old, same old. Big-city traffic, Monday morning smog, crowds, crime—endless crime. Damn, but he was tired of it.

Luke, his partner, was waiting for him up in Homicide. "You ain't gonna like this," Luke said, and he handed Mase a memo from their boss, telling Mase to meet him at ten sharp in the D.A.'s office.

Mase groaned. "You know what this is about?" he asked Luke.

"Nah. But I can guess."

So could Mase. He got to the D.A.'s and, sure enough, there was billionaire Richard Metcalf's attorney sitting at the big conference table with the D.A., Mase's captain, the court stenographer and two assistant D.A.s.

"Sit down, Mase," the D.A. said, nodding toward an empty seat. "Coffee, a roll?"

"I've eaten, thanks," Mase said, fixing Metcalf's attorney, whom Mase had dubbed "Sleazebag," with a glare.

It was the usual bullshit meeting. Sleazebag had more questions concerning the deposition Mase had given some months ago. Everyone was present—as always—to posture, bluff and defend positions. Mase's deposition, which was the most detailed he'd ever given on a homicide case, lay on the table. It must have been two hundred typed pages, detailing the exact events of the night of Councilman Edwards's murder. Hell, Mase even recalled Sleazebag asking what Mase had eaten for dinner. Like it really mattered.

The attorney leaned forward, pushed his bifocals up his nose and began leafing through the deposition. He cleared his throat and looked up then, taking in the whole entourage. "I'm afraid," he said, "that in this entire sworn deposition, there isn't one thing that links my client to the demise—" Mase loved that, the *demise* "—of Councilman Edwards. If this is all you have, gentlemen, then I must go to the court and file a summary judgment, asking for a dismissal of the case. You don't have anything."

Mase growled under his breath.

The D.A. smiled. "Harvey, Harvey, Harvey," he said to Metcalf's lawyer, "don't tell me you called this meeting on the grounds that we don't have a case."

He laughed good-naturedly. "We have a watertight case and you know it. We've got Mase LeBow's deposition right here stating that he met Mr. Hank Berry, known to every crime-solving force in the Union as the Hitman, in the lobby of the councilman's apartment. We don't need rocket scientists on the jury to figure out what he was doing there."

Sleazebag looked up at the ceiling, shaking his head. "Circumstantial. Merely circumstantial evidence. And, I might remind you, you don't have this so-called Hitman in custody. He's pure fantasy as far as my client is concerned."

"Harvey," the D.A. said, "we not only have Mase's sworn statement, but we have a voice match on both the Hitman and Metcalf discussing the murder on our wiretap."

"An illegal wiretap," Sleazebag put in. "There's a motion in front of the judge about that even as we sit here. You ever hear of entrapment?"

The D.A. smiled again. "It was perfectly legal. You know it. We all know it."

And so it went all morning.

Mase sat listening to the banter, growing angrier by the second. He couldn't help wondering if Sleazebag knew about the threat to Joey. Maybe he had come up with the idea in the first place.

By the time the meeting was over, Mase was so hot under the collar he was ready to throttle Metcalf's attorney. It had been a total waste of time, nothing accomplished, just lawyers posturing. The attorney had called the meeting with one intent in mind: to rattle Mase.

Well, Mase was rattled.

All afternoon he played catch-up at his desk. Paperwork and more paperwork. And Luke was behind, too, because of Mase's absence. What a way to start out a week. The one good thing, the only thing keeping Mase going, was the knowledge that Joey was safe. Safe and happy.

Callie, he thought when he looked up from a file, Callie was caring for his son, keeping him out of harm's way, healing him at last from the hurt of losing his mother.

Callie...

He didn't get home till after eight that night. He was hot and tired, the starched white collar of his shirt limp and grimy, his mood foul, the house dark. And very empty.

He didn't see the note stuck under his front door until almost nine, when he thought to switch on the porch light.

Mase picked it up by the corner, carefully, a cop habit. And then he read it.

We know where your kid is.
Keep it in mind when you go to court.

That was it. Two short lines that were like a vise, tightly squeezing his heart.

He never thought out his actions. He hardly realized where he was or what he was doing until he was standing on the pillared front terrace of Metcalf's Denver Country Club home, pounding on the double oak doors.

It took some doing to get Metcalf there, and the butler was shaking when he finally fetched his master. But Metcalf appeared. He was clad in a summer white dinner jacket and black bow tie, his razor-cut gray hair gleaming in the lamplight on the terrace.

"LeBow?" Metcalf said mildly. "To what do I owe this honor? I'm afraid I'm entertaining…"

Before the handsome entrepreneur could finish, Mase had him jacked up against the oak doors, a forearm crushing his neck against the hardwood.

"You son of a bitch," Mase rasped. "If one hair on my son's head is harmed, one single hair, you're dead. Do you hear me, Metcalf?"

The man was gasping, barely struggling against Mase's superior strength.

"Do you hear me?"

Metcalf managed to blink as if to say yes, and suddenly Mase caught himself, realizing the man was actually choking. He let up on the pressure.

"Tell me you're listening," Mase spat out. *"Tell me."*

"I…I can hear you," Metcalf whispered hoarsely, and Mase let him go.

"I'm not joking," Mase said as he started to back away. "I will kill you. I'm not threatening you, either, you lowlife—I'm promising." And then Mase left.

He remembered driving home—only a few blocks. But the downscale neighborhood Mase lived in might as well have been on a different planet. He tried showering to calm down. He tried working out with his gym equipment in the cool basement. Nothing helped. He kept thinking he should call Callie and her folks and warn them, but part of him believed the note had been a bluff. How could the Hitman know where Joey was? Hell, Mase would have spotted a tail on Callie's pickup truck. There hadn't been one. No one except his boss knew about the Someday Ranch. Not even Luke knew the whole story.

It had to be a bluff.

The doorbell rang at eleven that night. Mase answered it in his pajama bottoms with his service revolver in hand. He was surprised to find his boss on the front steps. Then he realized what must have happened. *Metcalf.* The bastard had called a political friend.

"The mayor called me," his boss said. "The mayor just called my home and told me what you pulled, LeBow."

Mase let out a ragged breath and lowered his gun. "You want to come in? I can explain..."

But Al Coleman interrupted him. "No explanation necessary. I want your gun and badge, Mase. You're suspended from duty as of right now. I can't even say I'm sorry after the stupid stunt you just pulled."

Mase stared at the captain for a long moment, deciding whether or not to try to explain. At least show him the threatening note. In the end, though, he thought, *Screw it.*

"I quit," Mase said tightly.

The captain frowned. "Look, Mase," he said, "you don't have to quit. I'm sure a week's suspension, with pay, I might add, will satisfy the mayor and..."

"You aren't listening," Mase said. "I quit." And then slowly, trying to control the shaking in his hand, he closed the door. He stood there in the entranceway for a long time. He thought about his gun, still dangling from his fingers, and his badge, on the dresser, and he realized he should have turned them over to his boss. Made it real...final.

Finally he shrugged and squared his shoulders. *To hell with it,* he thought. He didn't owe them a damn thing.

CHAPTER ELEVEN

BY THURSDAY MORNING at the Someday Ranch, tents and sleeping bags, coolers and big cooking pots were piling up in the entrance to the barn.

It was gymkhana weekend, an annual event held in July at the ranch—the Thorne family's way of saying thank-you to the people of Lightning Creek for their support during the year.

The first gymkhana had taken place fifteen years ago. Callie, still a teenager in high school, had just read *National Velvet,* and been fascinated by the gymkhana described in it. She had begged her parents to sponsor one and they had agreed. People camped out in tents and there were cookouts. Simple games on horseback were organized for the children, and rodeo-type events for the better riders. The first gymkhana had been such a success that the following year everyone decided it should be an annual event.

It was a bit of a logistical nightmare to set up. Dozens of tents were needed for sleeping out, folding chairs and picnic tables had to be hauled to the campsite by the trout stream that ran through the lower forty on the Someday Ranch. Horses had to be trailered in, campfire stoves and barbecue pits set up. Everyone pitched in. The Roadkill Grill provided some of the food, the grocery store, too. The local Moose Lodge hauled in the tables and chairs, the rent-all shop provided the big tent, and the liquor store donated a keg of beer.

Callie was so busy contacting everyone with the reminder list of what they were to bring—and still doing her therapy sessions—that she almost forgot Mase hadn't called since the previous Sunday night.

Her mother, however, hadn't forgotten.

They were in the kitchen helping Francine bake for the gymkhana when Liz brought up the subject. "My, Mase hasn't called, has he."

Callie ignored her and took a sheet of cookies out of the big Vulcan oven. She burned the side of her hand. "Ouch."

"Run it under cold water, dear," Liz said mildly. "I wonder why he hasn't called."

"You'd think he'd want to talk to Joey," Francine added.

And on it went. Sylvia even showed up and joined the conversation.

"What do you think, Callie?" Liz finally asked.

Everyone paused, expectant.

Callie sighed. She might as well put an end to their wondering right now. "If you all really must know," she said, "there is nothing between us."

"Nothing happened in Denver?" Francine blurted out.

Callie narrowed her eyes. "No. Nothing happened. Mase and I don't think of each other in that way. We're just acquaintances with a mutual goal—to see Joey get better."

Even Liz was surprised. "Callie, honey, are you telling us that you stayed, well, at Mase's house and nothing…"

"That's exactly what I'm telling you. Now, can we

get back to work here? The whole town's going to
show up Saturday morning and I'd like to be ready.
Okay?''

But later, when Callie dropped into bed that night,
the same questions beat at her. Why *hadn't* anything
happened at his house? In the kitchen, in her black
nightie, she'd thought maybe... Well, his expression
had certainly seemed...

It came rushing back. His bare chest and strong,
muscled arms. The way his eyes had darkened with an
emotion she'd thought...

Callie sat up in bed and bit her lip. *Stop it, Thorne.*
This was getting her nowhere. Mase thought of her in
only one way, as a skinny country bumpkin, a weirdo
who believed in horses and magic. She was dumber
than dumb to dwell on it. And all that business about
him having some deep dark secret was her imagination
running wild. She *wanted* him to have a secret, and
that way she could tell herself he was preoccupied. The
pathetic truth was that he had no interest in her at all.

But worse, much, much worse, was the realization
she was falling in love. All this time, all these years,
and she was finally tumbling head over heels for a guy.

Trouble was, Mase was the wrong guy.

SHERIFF REESE HATCHER was in his office when Mase
found him. Mase hadn't planned to stop, but several
miles south of Lightning Creek he decided he would
be foolhardy not to at least let the local authorities
know what was going on. And Reese was the local
authority.

He stopped at the dispatcher's desk and spoke to the
lady on duty, who was reading *Family Circle* maga-
zine. ''Uh, sorry to interrupt,'' Mase said, ''but is Sher-

iff Hatcher in?'' He nodded toward the half-closed door with the stenciled sign, Sheriff, on it.

''Sheriff's in, mister. Who should I say…?'' She batted her eyelashes at him.

''LeBow, Mase LeBow from Denver.''

Hatcher must have overheard because the door swung open and he appeared. ''Come in, Mase, didn't expect you back so soon.''

Mase offered him his hand and then strode into the office. He hadn't expected to be back himself—not for a couple of weeks, anyway. But the pressure was on in Denver. His boss had been calling him twice a day since Monday night, asking him to reconsider and come back to work. Even the mayor had called. Mase was going nuts, finding himself suddenly unemployed and looking over his shoulder every two seconds, steeped in paranoia. There was Joey, too, though Mase was still pretty darn positive his son was safe. He couldn't help worrying, though. What if he'd misjudged the situation? So he'd packed his bags, called his folks to let them know what was going on, locked his house and driven off.

It had been so easy. He would have thought leaving Denver under a cloud would have been difficult at best. But, hell, he'd felt nothing but blissful relief.

''Sit—sit on down there, son,'' Reese Hatcher was saying, ''and tell me what's on your mind.''

Mase sat in the hard-backed wooden chair across from Hatcher's oak desk and began the tale from the very beginning, starting with the 911 call from the city councilman to last Monday night, when he'd threatened Richard Metcalf and gotten himself a big fat suspension. ''But I quit instead,'' Mase said.

''Just like that?''

Mase nodded. "Right there in my pj's with my gun in my hand."

Reese pursed his lips. "So now you're here. And I'm bettin you'd like me to keep my eye out here in town for that Hitman character."

"Hank Berry. Yes," Mase said. "I've got a picture of him from the FBI's Most Wanted list." He pulled the faxed copy from his pocket. "He's armed and dangerous. No fooling around with this guy."

Hatcher took the picture, looked at it, grunted.

"If you could keep your eye out and tell your deputies, too."

"Shouldn't be a problem, son," Reese said. Then he raised a brow and lowered his voice. "Say, you told the Thornes about this?"

Slowly, Mase shook his head. "They only know about the upcoming trial. Nothing else." He, too, spoke quietly, as if they were in some kind of conspiracy together.

"Not even Miss Callie?"

"Not even her. Especially not her. She, uh, well, Callie's kind of fanciful, if you get my meaning."

"Oh, yeah," Hatcher said.

"And I just thought it would be best if she were kept in the dark. God only knows the things she might start to imagine."

"Hmm," Hatcher said, considering. "Can't say as I blame you. Sometimes there are things the public just don't need to know. Better for 'em if they don't."

"Couldn't agree more."

"Still…" Hatcher rubbed his whiskered chin. "I can see where if someone like Miss Callie were to learn you'd kept this from her… Well, she might get a real burr under her saddle. Oh, yeah, I can see that."

Mase expelled a breath. "What would you have done, Sheriff?"

"Oh, same thing as you, boy, same thing."

They talked for some time that Friday, about law enforcement, about small towns and their unique problems—not the least of which was being on a first-name basis with everyone. Mase recalled their conversation the night he and Callie had gone to the movie, and he had a gut feeling Hatcher was circling a point he was trying to make. Mase let it go. If there was something on Reese's mind, he'd get around to it eventually.

"So when is this murder trial?" Hatcher finally asked.

"Opening arguments are scheduled to start next week," Mase said. "If I can lie low till then and keep Joey out of sight, I'm home free."

"Well," Hatcher said, rising and shaking Mase's hand again, "I'll do everything in my power to help."

"Thank you, Sheriff." As Mase left the office, he nodded at the lady dispatcher, who was reading again. He was feeling much, much better. Now all he had to do was get out to the Someday Ranch and face Callie. He still wasn't sure just how much he should tell her, though. He climbed into his car, started the engine and recalled something Hatcher had said. He'd suggested that if "Miss Callie" ever found out the truth, he could see her getting a real burr under her saddle.

As Mase drove around the bucking bronco in the center of town, he said aloud, "Now, there's an understatement if I ever heard one."

NO ONE, NOT EVEN REESE, had told Mase about the gymkhana.

When he turned into the long drive at Callie's ranch,

the road looked like a sepia photograph of the Great Dust Bowl of the 1930s. Clouds of dust hung in the still, hot air, obscuring his vision. He darn near had a head-on collision with a truck. What the heck was going on here? Why all the traffic?

He found out shortly after arriving at the main house. Joey, after giving him a big hug, told Mase all about the camping-out party and how everyone in the world was coming. Not once did Joey question why his dad was there, but Callie, emerging from the kitchen with flour smudges on her face and her T-shirt, sure asked. Oh, you bet she did.

Surprise spread across her features. "Mase? What on earth are you doing here? I thought..."

He wanted to unload, tell her everything—that he'd used her ranch to keep Joey safe, that he'd quit the police force, how bad he felt for lying all along to her and everyone here, when they'd all been nothing but warm and welcoming since the very first. He looked at Callie, the expectant innocence in those big eyes, the soft curve of her lips, the tilt of her head, and he ached to come clean, to draw her to his chest and whisper into that perfect shell-pink ear the whole truth.

Instead he chickened out.

He'd figured she was going to ask—not just why he'd suddenly appeared, but how he'd gotten the time off work. What he was afraid of was that if he told her he'd quit his job, she'd want to know every detail. And if he told her exactly why, then he'd be telling her all about the Hitman and the threats to Joey.

He couldn't do it. He especially couldn't right now, with everyone hurrying this way and that. Joey and Rebecca and Peter were running around, playing practically under his feet. Everyone was getting ready for this big weekend, *happily* getting ready. No. Now was not the moment.

"Mase?" she was saying.

"I...got some time off," he muttered, gazing down at her, at those endearing flour smudges.

"Time off? You mean a vacation?"

"Something like that."

"Well... This is great. I mean, we didn't expect you."

"I should have called."

But Callie shook her head. Still, she was staring at him, puzzled, disbelieving. "No, this is fine," she finally said. "And to tell the truth, Dad and Jarod could sure use the extra hand. There's a ton of stuff to be loaded in the pickups and hauled out to the campsite. You don't mind...?"

Mase was delighted to help out. Nevertheless, when he left to find Tom and Jarod, he was aware of the assessing look Callie gave him.

I should have told her, Mase thought, his stomach knotting. It was too late, though, the damage was already done. But, oh man, was she going to hate him when the truth came to light. She'd probably never speak to him again.

Mase strode up to Tom, who was moving bales of hay to be loaded into the back of their pickup, and he thought about how Callie might very well tell him to get lost, and his guilt was replaced by a sudden stab of regret. He didn't know what direction his life was going to take now. He couldn't see the future beyond getting through the trial and keeping Joey safe. But the thought of losing Callie... When had that happened? When had she come to mean so much in his life?

Tom was as surprised to see Mase as anyone. He

took the red-and-white kerchief off his neck, mopped his face and stared at him. "Callie didn't say anything about you coming. I had the impression Joey was going to be here for a while longer."

Mase met Tom Thorne's eyes, and another dagger of guilt plunged into his belly. How many people was he going to deceive? He'd told Reese Hatcher the truth. Why didn't he trust this honest, hardworking rancher?

"Joey is staying, if that's all right," he began. He kept meeting Tom's questioning gaze. The dagger was still in his gut, twisting. "I'd like to stay for a while myself," he said.

"Hmm," Tom replied. "Why is it I get this feeling you're in some kind of a fix, son?"

A long moment passed, and finally Mase whistled between his teeth and absently rubbed his mustache with a hand. "I am in a bit of a mess," he said.

"I see." Tom was waiting.

Mase nodded, as if to say he wanted to take a walk, get out of Jarod's earshot. "You got a minute?"

"I've got all the time you need," Tom replied.

They walked together toward the riding ring, past stacks of ice chests and coolers and folded tents and tables and chairs awaiting transport. Mase knew he couldn't tell Tom everything. He could, however, stop lying. "I quit the police force," he stated, hands in his jeans pockets, his muscles tense.

"You quit?"

"Yes," Mase said, "and I'd like to tell you more, Tom, but I just can't right now. There were some problems. Still are. That's all I can say."

"I see," Tom said, leaning his sun-browned forearms on the top rail of the fence. "I guess if you could say more you would."

Mase nodded slowly.

"But I'd like to know if you quit under some sort of a cloud, son. I'm only prying because of my daughter," Tom continued carefully. "You understand?"

"Yes, I do," Mase said. "And I assure you, Tom, my quitting isn't because of anything I did wrong. I can return to the job if I want. The thing is, I don't *want* to. This has been coming for a while. I guess I just didn't see it. I'll tell you, I'm damn relieved to be out of it."

"I see," Tom said. "But I still get this feeling it's not entirely over. I mean, that there's something else…"

"There is, and I'm sorry, but I can't involve you."

Tom turned and gave Mase a long look. "Okay," he said, "I'll accept that. I just don't want Callie hurt. I take it she doesn't know what's going on?"

"She doesn't know a thing, Tom. Not even that I quit. I'd like to keep it that way, too."

"Bad idea," Tom said under his breath.

And Mase had to concur. "It might be the worst idea I've ever had."

It was a long afternoon of hard work. Mase, Tom, Jarod and several neighboring ranchers made a dozen trips to the campsite, unloading, driving back to the barn, loading up again. And it was unusually hot out. The kids didn't seem to mind, though. They ran around underfoot, excited. Supplies kept coming from town, and inside the main house, neighboring women pitched in, cooking and baking and marinating the chilled meats. Even the ranch's guests were put to work. James gathered tack in the barn, and Hal took inventory of everything that was driven to the campsite. Marianne and Linda helped Hal, making labels for the coolers, sleeping bags and tents. Even the horses, who had the day off, hung their heads over the fences, watching the whole affair with equine curiosity. Tomorrow they'd all get a good workout during the games. Beavis and Butt-Head simply hung around waiting for a bag of potato chips to get broken and spill in the dust. It was too much to hope for a cooler full of hamburger patties to topple.

At one point, led by Peter, of course, the kids became so rambunctious that Mase stepped in to quiet them down. Evidently, Peter had gotten hold of Liz's garden hose behind the house and was spraying Joey and Rebecca. Joey was having the time of his life, but Rebecca had put her hands over her face and gone rigid.

"Peter," Mase said sternly, "turn the hose off now."

"Daddy, no," Joey cried, "we're having fun. Mrs. Thorne doesn't mind."

"Maybe not," Mase said, taking the nozzle from Peter, "but Rebecca is a little girl, and she doesn't want to roughhouse like this."

"She doesn't mind," Peter insisted.

"Now, Peter," Mase said, crouching down to meet him eye to eye, "she can't really tell us if she minds, can she?"

"Rebecca's going to talk," Peter said suddenly, his face expressionless, his body utterly still.

Mase frowned. "I'm sure you're right, son, but right now she can't."

Peter appeared to come out of his spell and he only shrugged, as if Mase were speaking a foreign language.

The children finally found a new game, throwing an old, chewed-up tennis ball for the dogs, and Mase rewound the hose, placing it back on its holder against the house. He straightened and dusted himself off, and that was when he noticed Callie standing behind the screen door leading to the pantry. She was watching him.

He nodded to her. "The kids were getting too wild, soaking themselves."

She smiled a little. "No big deal. Those kids…" Her voice trailed off.

There was something in her expression, Mase thought. Curiosity? he wondered. And then he had it. It was disappointment. Callie knew he was lying to her, using her, and she was disappointed in him.

Mase flinched and turned away. There it was again, that knife digging in his gut, going deeper and deeper, as if his very soul were being cut away.

CHAPTER TWELVE

THE GYMKHANA WEEKEND was Callie's favorite occasion—better than Christmas and New Year's and the Fourth of July all rolled into one. She got to show off what her patients could do, what they had learned and how much they'd improved. The townsfolk came for the outing, as did many of the patients' family members.

It was always crazy. Lots of hard work and logistical problems. And Callie crossed her fingers each year for dry weather.

But this year, she thought, this year was special. Mase was there.

She wasn't positive how she felt about his sudden appearance yesterday. She was thrilled. But she was suspicious, too. That story he'd told her about a vacation… She didn't believe it for an instant. Yet he was there. And she hadn't stopped thinking about him. She couldn't. He worried her and made her furious, and she was dying to find out what secrets he was keeping from her. But there was no time. It was Saturday morning. She was simply too busy. If she got a moment, though, just one stolen moment to be alone with him, she'd pry the truth from him.

The scene flew into her mind, complete in every detail, right in the middle of the turmoil of setting up camp.

There was Mase, lying on a rack in a dark, damp dungeon, and she was standing over him. She was dressed in some kind of long flowing medieval dress and she commanded him to confess. "No," he said bravely, and then Callie raised her hand and the hooded torturer started turning the crank, stretching Mase on the rack. "I'll tell. Stop, stop! I'll tell," Mase gasped, writhing in agony.

She was going to find out his secret. He was going to tell her! She gestured to the torturer to let up on the rack so Mase could talk. She watched him, saw his naked, sweaty chest heaving. She was waiting for his confession, he was opening his mouth, he was going to tell her…

Her fantasy ended with the crash of a pickup truck backing into a table piled high with kitchen supplies. The dank dungeon disappeared, and in a moment Callie was running around like a chicken with its head cut off, directing the games, setting up barrels for barrel racing, trying to figure out where half the tack was. Where was that list Hal had made?

Even as she raced around, gave orders, timed the barrel races and began the egg-on-the-spoon game, Callie was always aware of Mase. He was watching the race. He was sitting in the shade talking to the Browns, Rebecca's parents. But he was *there,* and no matter how preoccupied she was, their gazes kept meeting across the riding ring or the tables set up for lunch.

She couldn't escape his presence. She didn't want to. She couldn't even imagine the gymkhana without Mase. If was as if he'd always been there with her, a part of the ranch, the family, a part of the magic. Even when she spotted him talking rather intently to Sheriff Hatcher, she couldn't be too upset. A little hurt. But never angry at Mase. This was love. She knew it. It was love flitting inside her belly on butterfly wings, love that kept her sleepless. Was he really the wrong man? Could she be that stupid?

Mase was there, too, when Hal became the biggest success of the weekend. Hal wheeled his chair to the mounting block, was helped onto Milky Way, and competed in the egg-on-the-spoon contest. The riders held an egg on a spoon and walked around the ring, then trotted their mounts and then cantered, if anyone got that far without dropping the egg. Laughter and squeals of dismay rose in the air as the eggs dropped and splattered on the ground. The close contest between Marianne and Hal, the last two left, had Callie beaming. Hal was riding well, his balance so stable he trotted his horse, holding the spoon in one hand, the egg sitting on it precariously. Marianne finally dropped hers, and Hal was the winner. He grinned, he bowed to the crowd, then he began to dismount without help. *What?* Callie thought.

Everyone stopped applauding and turned silent. Jarod ran into the ring to help, but Hal waved him away. Milky Way stood still as a statue as Hal slid off, touching his feet to the ground. The crowd drew in a collective breath as he sagged, his knees giving way, then pulled himself up by the saddle horn and stood, actually *stood* by himself.

Callie felt tears prick her eyes as Hal held on to the saddle horn and clucked to the brown-and-white pinto. Milky Way took a step, slowly, carefully, and so did Hal, holding on for support but walking on his own two feet.

"Oh, my Lord," Callie whispered to herself, and she began clapping for Hal as he made his way slowly

across the ring. She heard someone else start clapping—Marianne—then others. Soon everyone was applauding, and the whistles and shouts of congratulation
were almost deafening.

Sweat stood out on Hal's forehead as he reached his
wheelchair and sank down into it. He was exhausted
but proud, so proud. His mother, who'd come all the
way from Kansas City, went over and hugged him,
laughing through her tears.

Callie walked up to Hal, but for a minute she
couldn't say anything past the lump in her throat.

"How'd I do, coach?" he asked.

"Not bad," Callie finally managed to say.

Then Marianne came over. She leaned down and
kissed Hal on the lips. It looked as if it were a pretty
familiar habit, too, and Callie wondered what had been
going on these past few weeks after lights-out.

But she couldn't stay there and scold Hal and find
out just when and how he'd accomplished this marvel.
She had a hundred things to do. Someone wanted to
know if another ice-run into town was needed, someone else asked if it was time to hide the items for the
scavenger hunt. Kahlua had thrown a shoe, Francine
needed more paper plates for dinner, and Sylvia was
nowhere to be found. Liz was helping two of the town
ladies set bait on fishing hooks near the trout stream,
and Tom was... Callie spotted her dad. He was talking
to Mase, nodding, and Mase was doing that thing with
his mustache, slowly smoothing it, and Callie knew he
was deep in thought. She guessed she'd have to take
care of Kahlua's shoe herself. But, darn it, was Mase
confiding something to her dad? Not knowing made
her crazy.

Lindsay Duncan and Rex Trowbridge were there,

representing the Lost Springs Ranch. They'd come in Lindsay's truck, hauling a horse for Lindsay to ride the next day in the games. Callie waved and called out a greeting to them, but Liz asked her a question just then and she had to figure out into what black hole the Thornes' sleeping bags had disappeared.

At dinner Callie got a chance to sit down and relax at last. Her duties were mostly over, and everything had gone pretty well so far. It hadn't rained, nor was it threatening to. She took a deep breath and got in line for barbecue.

When she sat down at the long table, Mase materialized beside her, a plate in hand.

"Mind if I join you?" he asked.

"My pleasure," she said.

"It's been quite a day."

"It always is." Callie picked up a succulent rib and began to nibble.

"That was really something with Hal."

"That kid," Callie said, shaking her head, "keeping it secret, pretending he couldn't feel anything."

"It was mostly you he wanted to do it for," Mase said.

She looked up at him in surprise. "You think so?"

"Yeah, I do."

"I kind of thought Marianne might have inspired him, if you know what I mean."

"I think you're selling yourself short."

His voice seemed to go through her and touch something deep inside. Those questions she wanted to ask, those answers she was going to pry out of him, everything flew from her brain, and all that was left was mush. *Come on, Thorne,* she thought, *you're acting like an airhead. The guy is deceiving you.* But he was so close to her, his arm practically brushing hers, the crisp golden hairs, the warmth— Despite herself, a sigh trembled along her limbs and settled deep in her stomach. She was lost. She tried to lick the barbecue sauce off her fingers but her lips wouldn't even work right.

"You're doing wonderful work," Mase said then.

"Oh, thanks," she managed to reply, and somehow she got through dinner.

After everyone had eaten and all the chores were done, the campfires were built up. The crowds gathered around, beers or sodas in hand, marshmallows stuck on sticks, and gradually the din settled. As hot as the day had been, jackets and down vests now appeared. This was Wyoming, after all, and the evenings cooled quickly. A few songs were sung, and more than a few stories told.

Each of Callie's patients stood and made a little speech about what they'd learned and how much Callie and Jarod had helped them. There were tears and laughter and everyone clapped, and Callie blushed crimson.

James presented both Callie and Jarod with gift certificates from all the patients. Although it was only mid-July, a few of the guests would soon be leaving. In six short weeks Jarod would go back to school, and everything would wind down. She always felt kind of nostalgic on this weekend, though she tried to think of the summer as a glass that was still half-full, not half-empty. Joey would be leaving at some point, too. Back to Denver. That fall he'd be in first grade, he'd told her proudly. For some reason, Callie felt terribly sad. What would Rebecca do without him?

She frowned and pondered the kids' relationship. Rebecca lived only ten miles from Lightning Creek, but Joey…Denver was so far away. If only Joey were in school here. If only, by some miracle, Mase would…

But she had no time to indulge in a fantasy right now, because she had to stand up by the campfire and give her own speech.

She slowly turned and looked at the circle of faces touched by firelight. "It's not me," she said, "it's you who do all the hard work. And the horses. I just talk, that's all, give you directions. I'll miss all of you who'll soon have to leave, but I hope you come back to visit or to work some more. I'll be here. I'll always be here.

"You've been wonderful. You've all come a long way. And thank you so much for the present and for the honor of working with you."

More applause. A few tears. Embarrassed, Callie wiped the moisture from her own eyes. Her heart was full as she returned to her place on the circle and sank down cross-legged on the ground.

"You lied," she heard from behind her.

"What?" She twisted around and there was Mase, light and shadow flickering on his handsome face.

"You lied. It *is* you," he said, and then he leaned close. "Let's go for a walk."

Mase did not have to twist her arm. She rose without answering, looking around to see who might be watching, and then she quietly followed him into the night.

They went out of camp, away from the firelight and noise and commotion, up a dry streambed between two hills. Overhead the sky was a black velvet cloak upon which diamonds had been spilled. And the coyotes were serenading a lopsided moon, yipping and screeching and singing off in the darkness.

"Nice," Mase said.

"Yes, nice," Callie replied, and the questions bubbled up inside her. If she asked him—even one single question—would she shatter the moment? She had to risk it. "Mase, what about the trial? Isn't it soon? I mean, do you know how long you'll be staying here?"

He took his time answering. "No."

"But the murder trial..."

"Callie," he said, his voice a caress, "I understand that there are things you want to know. You have to be wondering. I'd like to tell you. I want to tell you everything. I can't right now, though. Can you understand that?"

She could lie. But she wouldn't. "No," she breathed. "I'm not a child."

Mase laughed softly then, and he took her arm and guided them to a rocky outcrop, where they both sat down. A breeze stirred her hair, cool and pine-scented, and she reached up to tuck a stray strand behind her ear.

"Fall will come soon," she said, staring toward the distant peaks. "It's hard to believe now, but it will come so quickly...."

His shoulder was touching hers; she felt it not as a touch but as pure sensation, a firing of all the nerve cells in her skin, radiating out to the rest of her body and leaving her out of breath. Her skin prickled, and her heart sounded drumbeats in her ears.

She closed her eyes for a moment. "You don't trust me," she said, and she realized her voice was thick, her throat tight.

"Callie, I..." But he hesitated, and slowly shook his head.

She saw his hand, pale in the darkness, lying on his lap, and she couldn't stop herself from resting her fingers on it. "It…hurts me," she breathed. "I wish you would just trust me, Mase."

He turned his hand and captured her fingers, then his head tilted toward hers. "I do trust you," he whispered.

She wanted to say so much more, but her breath had stopped in her chest. She couldn't halt the inevitable. Not anymore. Oh, Lord, what was she doing?

His lips met hers. Featherlight. And his mustache tickled sweetly. She felt his hand move to the back of her head and cup it, and he drew her close. His breath was hot and quick now, and she let herself sink against his strong chest, the rise and fall of it matching her own.

His kiss deepened into her mouth, and she opened to him, a flower opening to the sun. Her arms went around him and he enfolded her tightly. She was lost in his scent, the feel of him, his strength, drowning in her own need, and an ache was building deep inside.

They drew apart for a moment and searched each other's face, their features shadowed in the darkness, their eyes locked in passion. Then they came together with sighs and murmurs, and she ran her hands down his back, tracing his ribs, up to his neck and the thick hair above it.

Mase eased her onto her back and stretched out next to her, his body so close that she felt a sudden shock of awareness at how easily, how perfectly they fit together. He kissed her, his fingers resting lightly on her neck then moving downward, tentative yet knowing, and she sighed against his lips. He caressed her breasts through her clothes, cupping them, and she wanted to tear the material away as she strained against him.

"Oh, Mase," she whispered, "oh, yes."

She could feel his hardness, he was pressed so

tightly against her, and tremors of longing moved in waves up her limbs. She was so happy, so blissfully happy.

And then, abruptly, he sat up.

Callie felt as if the earth had fallen away beneath her.

"No," he breathed. "This isn't what you want."

"Mase…"

"No, Callie. It's not fair to you. I shouldn't have done that."

"But I…I wanted you to, Mase. I…"

Suddenly he stood, and she heard him swear. "I said *no*. I'm sorry, Callie, this was my fault, and it's all wrong." He shook his head wordlessly, angrily, and her heart sank into an abyss. What awful secret held him in its grasp? Was it something about his wife? Was he still in love with his dead wife?

Callie would have asked, begged, wheedled an answer out of him. She didn't care what it might cost her, but she never had the chance, because just then a scream, a thin, distant wail, rose from the direction of the campsite.

She and Mase looked at each other, frozen for a heartbeat of time, and then suddenly they were both running, scrambling down the dry streambed toward the camp. When they reached the edge of the firelight, they could see people rushing around aimlessly, confused.

Callie went straight to the tents housing the kids— one for the boys, another for Rebecca and Marianne— and found Sylvia and her mother there. They had both flashlights and a lantern lit, and were inside the girls' tent, crowded around Rebecca.

"She had a nightmare," Marianne was explaining

breathlessly. "It woke me up because she was crying in her sleep, so I got up, and then she awoke and started to scream. Oh, wow, it scared me! She screamed and I jumped, and then I realized she'd said something. I mean she actually *talked*."

Callie gasped. "What? What did she say?"

But Marianne didn't need to reply, because Callie heard Rebecca's voice herself, a little girl's voice, sobbing, "Joey, I want Joey."

"Oh, dear Lord," Callie whispered, and she pushed her way through the women gathered around Rebecca.

"Get Joey," she said, turning toward the tent flap, where a crowd had gathered. "Someone get Joey."

Liz was holding Rebecca on her lap, stroking the little girl's hair and crooning to her. "It's all right, honey, it was just a bad dream. Joey's coming. Don't worry, he's coming. You're fine. Everything's okay."

Callie kneeled down beside Rebecca and took the child's hand. "He's coming, sweetheart. Don't cry. Hey, kiddo, can you say his name again?"

"Joey," Rebecca wailed.

"Oh, my goodness," Sylvia said in an awed tone. "She's talking. She's really talking."

The Browns arrived then, rushing into the tent, wild-eyed, jackets hastily thrown on over sleepwear. "What is it?" Rebecca's mother, Leslie, asked, her face ashen.

"Is she all right?" Her father, Dennis, stood there, equally distraught.

"She's fine," Liz said. "She had a nightmare, that's all."

Rebecca's mother sank down on the tent floor and gathered her daughter in her arms. "Oh, my poor baby."

"She spoke," Liz said quietly to the Browns. "She wants Joey. She said his name."

"What?"

"Yes."

"She did, really? My God," Leslie said. "Sweetheart, can you talk to your mommy?"

"Joey," Rebecca said. "Where's Joey?"

The boy appeared at the door of the tent just then, sleepy-eyed. Mase had a hand on his son's shoulder, and they pushed through the throng into the crowded tent.

"Here he is," Mase said.

"Rebecca," Joey said, yawning. "I was asleep."

"Joey," the little girl sobbed. But she quieted down, hiccupping once and taking a deep, heartbreakingly ragged breath.

"You want to play?" Joey asked, not quite awake. "Isn't it kinda late?"

Callie couldn't help smiling. A titter of suppressed laughter ran through the gathered crowd.

"She had a bad dream, Joey," Liz explained. "She was frightened."

"Oh," he said.

"Joey. I want..." Rebecca struggled for words.

"What do you want, honey?" Liz asked.

"Joey sleep here," she said.

"She's talking." Dennis Brown's voice was filled with wonder.

Rebecca's mother bent her head down onto her daughter's golden curls and cried. "Yes, he can sleep here. Okay, Joey?"

"Sure. I just gotta get my sleeping bag. What was your dream about, Rebecca?"

"It was scary."

"Oh," Leslie breathed. "Oh my goodness."

By the time Callie and Rebecca's parents got the children settled and everyone else cleared out of the tent, it was very late. All the adults were too hyped to sleep, so they built up the campfire and talked, discussing Rebecca's breakthrough.

"I think keeping things as normal as possible is best," Callie suggested. "Don't make a big fuss, just accept it. The way Joey did."

"You don't want to make her self-conscious," Sylvia added. "She's a very sensitive kid."

"My little girl," Rebecca's mother said. "I can't believe it."

"Who would have guessed it would take another kid?" Tom Thorne mused.

"Not just any kid," Jarod said. "It took Joey. They have some kind of special bond."

"I don't care what it took or who or how, I only care that it worked. Whatever it was," Dennis said.

"Amen," James put in.

The discussion went on until, one by one, people drifted away to their tents. It was dreadfully obvious to Callie that Mase was avoiding her, and her emotions were torn asunder; on one hand she was ecstatic about Rebecca speaking, and on the other, she was deeply troubled by Mase's reaction to a thing as simple, as natural as their kiss.

Eventually she climbed into her sleeping bag in the tent she was sharing with Sylvia and Francine. The two other women were still awake, talking quietly about Hal and Rebecca and the wonderful events of the day.

"Well," Sylvia said, "I sure hope Rebecca doesn't have a relapse, because eventually Joey will leave for home."

"Oh, my," Francine whispered, "I hadn't thought of that. What do you think, Callie?"

"Huh?"

Francine repeated her question.

"Oh, oh, I don't know. We'll figure something out," Callie whispered absently.

The two women chatted in whispers for a while and then finally drifted off to sleep. So did Callie. But sometime in the wee hours she woke up with a start, positive something, *someone,* was on top of her. It was so hot, heavy…Mase? But it was only her tangled sleeping bag. She unzipped it and sat up, mopping at the sweat on her neck and chest. The dream she'd been having rushed back—she and Mase, making love. His hands, his mouth, the length of him possessing her.

She kicked away the bag and muttered to herself.

"Callie? Are you okay?" came Francine's groggy voice.

"No," Callie whispered harshly. "I can't sleep. I…I want something and I…I can't have it."

"Chocolate," Francine murmured. "Have some chocolate." Then she was snoring lightly again.

Chocolate, Callie thought. *I wish.*

CHAPTER THIRTEEN

SUNDAY WAS ANOTHER tumultuous day of events at the Someday Ranch gymkhana. Reese Hatcher, in his annual performance, won the adult barrel racing with his aged gelding, Mr. Macho. Jarod led a hike of all children ten and older, with Peter as his right-hand man. Callie watched them go with pride and a little bit of yearning. She'd love to be hiking with them, leaving the pandemonium of the camp behind. Leaving Mase LeBow behind.

His politeness was agonizing and wounded her more than rudeness or anger. She'd melted in his arms last night, kissed him with abandon, and he'd kissed her back. Now here he was, smiling distantly, saying, "Would you like these tables set up over there?" as if he were a stranger. All morning he had helped set things up, and they were together, of necessity, but his infuriating courtesy never wavered.

Callie was distracted and she kept having her crazy, dreamlike visions. In the middle of setting up orange cones in the riding ring for the kids' agility contest, a fantasy came out of nowhere.

She was eating lunch with the whole crew—crispy fried chicken, potato salad, sliced tomatoes—and everyone was chatting about what a great gymkhana it had been, when Mase stood before her, his eyes dark with passion. She put her plate down and faced him.

He pushed her onto the lunch table, scattering food, knocking over drinks, scrunching up the paper table-cloth, but neither of them cared. He was on top of her, kissing her, and suddenly no one was around, no kids, no parents, no horses, and he was whispering in her ear....

"Callie, what time is the agility class? What time, Callie? I'm back from the hike already. Do I have to get my horse yet?" Peter's voice intruded on her fantasy and it went up in a puff of smoke.

"What? Oh, Peter, it's in, let's see, an hour. Yes, go find Cinderella and start getting ready. Tell Joey and Rebecca, too. And the Sanderson kids from town."

"Okay, Callie, I'll do it. I'll find everyone. Think I'll win, Callie? Am I good enough?" Peter demanded with rapid-fire delivery.

Callie thought of Peter's unusual ability to foresee the future and almost smiled at his uncertainty now. But he was becoming overexcited, so she took hold of his arm, a signal to him to concentrate, to listen. "You were right," she said, "about Rebecca. That was pretty special, Peter."

"No one ever believes me," he said with a pout. "I'm always right."

"*I* believe you, Peter, you know that."

"Yeah, Callie, you do, you believe me."

"Go on now, find the kids and tell them to get hopping."

She looked after Peter as he ran—he never walked—to locate the other youngsters, and she smiled after him, but her lips went stiff as soon as she spotted Mase again. He was standing in the shade under one of the few trees, talking to Dennis and Leslie Brown. He leaned a shoulder against the tree, and his arms were crossed as he listened to something Rebecca's mother was saying. Joey and Rebecca were teasing Beavis and Butt-Head nearby.

What were they discussing? Callie wondered. Rebecca's newfound power of speech, no doubt, or maybe how to get their kids together once school started. Something important, she was sure. Mase looked serious as he listened, his dark brows drawn together, but then Rebecca screeched at something Beavis did. "Stop it, you dog!" she said. Callie could hear it, too, even from where she was. And Mase and the Browns turned and watched, and they looked so darn happy. Even Mase grinned, seeming carefree and young. Sadly, Callie realized he'd never looked like that with her. Not once. When he was with her he looked tortured, or at best faintly amused. But never happy.

She turned away, unable to bear his lighthearted response to everyone and everything except her. *Oh, shut up,* Callie told herself. *Quit whining, Thorne.*

The kids were wonderful in the agility contest, guiding their horses in a serpentine pattern between the cones, then around the end one. They couldn't miss any or knock one over, and they were timed.

Hal and Marianne were there to watch, and Hal stood, steadying himself on a cane, taking slow, careful steps. Marianne never left his side, seemingly as proud as he was. Callie wondered more than once if Marianne had been in on the plan all along.

Callie's friend Twyla tapped her on the shoulder. "Aren't they having fun?" she asked. "Isn't it great?"

Callie turned around and smiled at the redheaded hairdresser. "They sure are. Did you just get here, Twyla?"

"Afraid so. I promised to give Doreen Kovac a perm this morning. It was an emergency."

Callie rolled her eyes, and they both laughed.

"Come in for a trim next week," Twyla said. "Your hair's beginning to look straggly." And she wandered off.

One of the kids from town won the agility contest, Peter came in second, and Joey got a prize for most improved. He glowed with pride as he held his ribbon up for everyone to see. Mase stuck his thumb up in a victory gesture and Joey did the same.

After lunch began the laborious process of packing up the entire camp and returning everything to town or the ranch. Everyone was tired and dusty and sunburned, the normal outcome of the weekend.

Some of the families were driving home or to the airport in Casper, but a few would spend the night. The Browns were staying for a while, trying to decide on how to part Rebecca and Joey when the time inevitably arrived.

People flowed in an unending stream to congratulate Callie and her folks and the ranch staff. Callie smiled and joked and thanked every single person, from Sheriff Hatcher to Rory Reilly, the feed-store owner's ten-year-old son, who'd brought a big bag of horse cookies from his dad's store.

It was wonderful. Callie loved the exhausting weekend, she adored every last person who showed up to help out, and she was thrilled about Hal and Rebecca and all the rest of her patients, who worked so hard and repaid her faith in them a hundredfold. She was crazy about the kids, and proud of all the work done by Jarod, Sylvia and Francine. And of course her folks.

She moved within a haze of fatigue and utter contentment. Except for one fly in the ointment.

That tall, dark and handsome cop over there.

She wanted to treat Joey like a family member, but she felt constrained by his father's presence. If she showed Joey her love, would Mase think she was only trying to butter him up? Did he resent her closeness to his son?

How long was he staying, anyway? He'd said he couldn't tell her what was going on, that she'd have to trust him.

Trust him?

Did he have some awful, deep dark secret? Had he done something illegal? She could hardly imagine Mase doing anything like that. Did it have something to do with his job? Was he an undercover cop, in some kind of danger? The questions were always there, battering away at Callie. Sometimes they made her sad, sometimes mad as heck, sometimes hopeless, but always on edge, not quite herself. Damn Mase, she thought at regular intervals. Why had he come back?

If he stayed, even for a few days, she'd see him at the house, at meals, with Joey, talking to her dad. Always *there*, in her heart and in her mind, and she wouldn't be able to get a moment's respite.

There were still a lot of trips needed to move everything from the campsite. The work would continue on Monday and part of Tuesday, too, but Callie stayed at the ranch that afternoon to take care of the horses.

All the men were busy ferrying and unloading pickups, so she and her mom fed the horses in the barn, then, with Peter's help, turned them out to pasture.

Callie brushed her hands on her thighs. "There, done. Thanks for the help."

"Another year." Liz sighed. "Wow, they go by fast."

"I'm starved," Callie said.

"I think Francine's just putting out cold cuts and things. The kitchen's torn apart, and you know how upset she is until everything's shipshape again."

They walked back to the house, Peter running circles around them, the sun resting low on the hills. Callie and Liz discussed how many people would be staying, and Callie cringed inwardly when Mase's name came up.

Liz studied her daughter. "So, what's with you two?" she finally asked.

Callie gave what was meant to be a light, trilling laugh, but it came out wrong, so she coughed instead.

"Well?"

"Nothing," Callie said. "There's nothing with us. Nothing at all."

"Methinks the lady doth protest too much," Liz said.

"Give it a break, Mom."

"If you like him, honey, then why don't you just…"

"*Mom.*"

"Okay, okay."

He was there, in the house, eating a light meal with the Browns, when Callie and Liz got back.

Callie smiled politely and looked longingly at the buffet of meat and cheese, fruit and vegetables, dips. Yum, Francine's curry dip. But she excused herself to take a shower and change, hoping against hope that Mase would be gone when she came downstairs again to eat.

He was still there, of course, talking to Tom and Jarod, who'd given up heavy labor for the day.

Callie filled her plate, sat down next to Linda and her visiting husband and ate her dinner, making small talk with the couple.

"What's with you two?" Linda finally said, gesturing toward Mase across the room.

"What?"

"Anyone can see it from a mile away," Linda said. "Did you have a lover's quarrel?"

"Oh, Lord," Callie moaned. "There's nothing going on between us. Why is everybody being so darn nosey?"

"Don't worry, you'll work it out," Linda said. "True love conquers all."

"You're a hopeless romantic," her husband said fondly.

"Excuse me," Callie muttered. "I really have to…" She searched her mind frantically. "Well, you know, I have to…um…go."

She went outside to escape the stultifying atmosphere, the tension, the veiled looks and the alarming notion that everyone in the house—*everyone*—was talking about her and Mase. She walked down the porch steps, down the flagstone path and across to the barn, empty now but for the sweet lingering smell of horses and alfalfa.

She hugged herself and sat on a bale of hay, trying to put Mase out of her head. She tried to think of something else, anything else, but he stubbornly rose in her mind's eye, blotting everything else out. His dark hair, the errant lock on his forehead, heavy brows over deep blue eyes. Mustache, lips, strong chin with a hint of a cleft.

Callie sat there and closed her eyes; her lips held the

memory of his kiss, and she could feel the phantom embrace of his arms around her.

Oh, dear Lord, if only it were real.

BY MONDAY MORNING, MASE couldn't bear Callie's nearness another moment. He had not slept well and had no appetite, not even for Francine's food. He couldn't forget for one moment how Callie had felt in his arms, soft skin and womanly curves and fragrant, silky hair. He couldn't forget the changing expressions of her face, the way she chewed her lip and frowned, the way her hands flew about in graceful gestures. And when he shut his eyes, he still saw the beautiful moonlit dew in her gaze before their lips met.

But mostly he felt her presence. Her spirit and her overwhelming love, her energy, the way she inspired people. The nice way she cured every malady that came within her magic circle.

Hal, Rebecca, Joey. All the rest, too. Their results were perhaps less spectacular, but their achievements were no less extraordinary. Each and every human being on the ranch was better off because of Callie Thorne.

But she was merely polite to him, avoiding him whenever she could. He'd hurt her feelings, acted like a real jerk. He couldn't play those kinds of games with women; he hadn't had any practice in years. He'd made some pretty bad mistakes with Callie.

He never should have touched her, that was the biggest mistake. A whopper. And now he couldn't think when he was around her. He sweated, his stomach tightened. He wanted to tell her the whole story, why he'd lied to her, why he had to do it. How afraid he was for Joey. But even if he did tell her, it was too

late now; she'd never forgive him. Even her dad had
hinted at a less-than-satisfactory outcome.

After breakfast Mase asked Tom if he could have
the morning off. He'd be back later to help move
things.

"I have to go into town and make some calls. I don't
want to do it here," he lied.

"Sure, I understand. Listen, you can do whatever
you want, son. You're not employed here, you know."

"Maybe I should be," Mase muttered.

He drove into Lightning Creek, pulled up in front of
the sheriff's office and got out of his car. Inside, he
said hello to the lady dispatcher, whose name plaque
read Donna Knudson.

"Hi," she replied.

"You must be the only dispatcher working here,"
Mase noted.

"The law never sleeps," she said, smiling impishly,
"nor can it afford too many employees."

"Ain't that the truth," Mase agreed. "Sheriff
Hatcher around, Donna?"

"You know what, I do believe he's down the road
at the grill having a cup of the stuff they call coffee."

"Think he'd mind if I joined him?"

"I think he'd be happy to see you, Mr. LeBow,"
she said, flirting.

He had coffee with Reese Hatcher, and for a few
minutes they rehashed the weekend.

"You were pretty darn good on that horse," Mase
commented.

"Aw, he's so smart, done it so many times, he could
round those barrels without me on his back. And no
one'd dare win that contest. Scared to death of me."

Hatcher laughed. "But that's one great weekend, ain't it?"

"Yeah, it was great." Mase hesitated, then continued, "I take it you haven't seen anyone fitting the description of the Hitman."

"Sure haven't, but I've got his picture up in the office and all my deputies alerted. Hell, a man like that'd stick out like a sore thumb in this county."

"I'm probably nuts, worrying about him showing up here. There's no way he could know where Joey is."

"Every parent worries about his kids, nothing wrong with that."

Mase shook his head. "It's just that I've seen too many bad things, too much evil. I'm a classic case of cop burnout."

"Stick around, son, and breathe the country air. It'll cure what ails you."

Mase considered buying some flowers for Callie, a nice bouquet, and apologizing, but when he really chewed it over, it seemed silly. He'd have to tough it out without props, he guessed. He got in his car and drove back out to the ranch, empty-handed.

No one was around. Mase discovered Liz and Francine in the main house. Liz was doing laundry and Francine was grumbling about a missing spatula. "I won't be able to cook. Not one thing. I just know it's laying out there in the dust at the campsite. I just know it."

Mase poked his head into the kitchen. "Have you seen Joey?"

"They've all gone on a wildflower walk."

"Who...?"

Francine narrowed her eyes at him, too busy looking for her spatula to be bothered. "Sylvia and the Browns

took all the kids on a nature walk or some blamed
thing. Hal and Marianne are in her room playing
cards.'' Francine snorted at that. ''And Tom and Jarod
are dropping tents and stuff at some of the neighbors'
places.''

''Hmm,'' Mase said. ''And Callie?'' He couldn't believe he asked.

It was Liz who answered. She stuck her head around
the corner of the pantry and said, ''She's sorting out
the tack in the barn. I'll bet she could use a hand.''

Mase only nodded. He knew Callie had everything
under control. She always did. He climbed the stairs to
the guest room where he was staying and stood in the
doorway. He could catch some shut-eye. Read a little
and close his eyes for a precious few minutes. He *could*
do that. He was tired; they were all tired. Sure, a nap.

Instead, he found himself at the door to the tack
room. *Big mistake* ran through his head, but it was too
late to back off now.

Callie turned and saw him. Her face brightened then
darkened, and she went back to sorting out the bridles.

He cleared his throat. ''Liz said you might need
some help.''

Lord, but she looked lovely in the golden light of
afternoon, those dust motes dancing around her hair,
the smell of alfalfa sweet and fresh. Somewhere a horse
whinnied softly and nudged a wooden gate, and in the
rafters the barn swallows cooed and darted.

''Well?'' Mase said. ''Can I give you a hand?''
There was a dryness in his throat. He swallowed.

''Everything's all set,'' Callie told him, still busying
herself. She was wearing old jeans and sandals today,
no boots and a western-cut plaid shirt that had seen
better days. Her sleeves were haphazardly pushed up,

the collar turned up on one side. The V in the front of it was deep, and he could just make out the small, firm roundness of her breasts. No way was she wearing a bra.

She bent over then, picked something up, raised a forearm to her brow and dried it. Something inside Mase twisted hotly.

"I'm no damn good at games," he said. "I never was. I was going to buy you flowers, ask you to forgive me for being such a jerk. But it's a lie. What I really want to do is kiss you."

"Oh," she whispered, her face averted. "Wow."

He stared at the tilt of her chin, the loose strands of golden hair, the way she held herself, erect, alert, as skittish as one of her colts.

Without another word, he stepped toward her. "Callie," he said, his eyes darkening, "turn around."

He saw her stiffen, as if preparing for flight. But she didn't move.

"Callie," he said again, "look at me."

"No," she said, but there was no conviction in her voice.

"Turn around."

Slowly, fighting herself, she came around toward him. There couldn't have been three feet between them. It seemed a chasm too wide to cross for an instant, and then he saw it in her eyes, the desire, a mirror of his own.

Mase crossed the space between them in a single stride and stood looking down at her, his fists balled at his sides. "If you tell me no," he said in a hoarse voice, "I'll go right now. It's your call."

The terrible struggle inside her played across Callie's face, beautiful and sincere and so very uncertain. "I...I do want you," she finally breathed. "But I…I need to know…"

"This is all you need to know," he said, and he took her in his arms and crushed her to him. "Last chance, Callie," he warned, his heart crashing against his ribs. "Tell me to go or ask me to stay."

"Stay," she moaned, "stay with me," and he could hear the trepidation and longing in her voice.

It didn't matter. He'd wipe that uncertainty away.

He kissed her. His arms still imprisoning her, he bent his head to hers and took her mouth in a hard kiss that sent shock waves through his limbs. He felt her instant response, the trembling need in her, the way her slim fingers curled into the back of his shirt, opening and closing. Her thighs were pressed into him, and he could feel searing warmth burst from her.

He kissed her long and hard and thoroughly, probing the sweetness of her mouth, feeling the hardness of her nipples against his chest. He half lifted her then, until her toes barely touched the floor, and his hands slid beneath her loose shirt, up her back, stroking the smooth skin, kneading it. She sighed against his mouth, and he drew her heated body hard against his.

"The loft," Mase said thickly, easing his hold on her.

"Yes, the loft," she whispered.

"Will anyone…?"

Callie shook her head. "We have hours."

Hours, he thought.

They climbed the short ladder to where the bales of winter hay were stored. The swallows darted through the thin shafts of light piercing the dimness. Callie took his hand and found a path. He could feel the heat of her, even in her fingers.

"Here," she said, and she turned to him, laying her hands on his chest. Her eyes were moist, and her breath was coming as rapidly as his.

And then he froze.

"Mase? What is it?"

"I don't have any...protection," he said, suddenly sober.

But she only smiled. "It's okay. I'm irregular, and I take the pill. As for the other stuff, I'm okay. Are you...?"

"I'm fine," he said. "I haven't been with anyone since..." But Callie silenced him with a finger to his lips. He put a hand on either side of her head and stared at her for a very long moment. Then he said, "You are so damn beautiful," and his mouth found hers again.

It was Callie who undid the buttons on his shirt and peeled it off him, their mouths still clinging. And it was Callie who removed her own shirt. His heart pounded once, painfully strong, before it settled back into a rhythm as he held her away from him and gazed at the firm roundness of her breasts.

Tentatively, Mase touched her nipples with both hands. Her head lolled to one side and she made a small sound in her throat. They were still standing, and a shaft of light fell across their shoulders. When Mase moved his hands, the golden light spilled across her breasts, softly illuminating her like a painting from the hand of an old master.

Mase eased her down onto the hay and helped her discard her jeans. She lay there now in only her panties, seductively delicate with the slim curve of her hips and thighs, her arms half covering her breasts.

He stared longingly at her while he shrugged off his own jeans and lay beside her. Then, with one hand, he took both of hers and held them above her head, not forcefully, but gently. His other hand found a breast, and with one finger he teased the soft peak until it rose in a firm nub.

Callie's head rolled to the side and she gave a soft cry, arching toward him, toward his touch. He leaned over and tenderly put his lips to her breast and drew the hardened peak against his teeth, playing with her, delighting in the moans his touch produced.

He took his time, kissing first one breast and then the other, slowly bringing Callie to a fevered pitch. He kissed the pulse at her neck and found her mouth, then went back to her breasts again, his hand cupping the firmness to his mouth as he drew her in.

When he finally let her hands go, it was only long enough to ease her panties down. And then he was out of his own pants, his long muscles pressed to hers.

He kissed her mouth again and then raised himself above her, gently opening her thighs with a nudge from a knee. He felt his hardness pressed to her soft, warm folds, and she shifted slightly beneath him, ready. He entered her slowly. Raised up on his hands, his eyes holding hers, he pressed gently into her and heard her sharp intake of breath as he reached her core. Her fingers were on his back, digging into him, and her hips rose against his own, urging him on.

For a long, torturous minute, Mase remained utterly still, poised above her, deep, deep inside her, and then he began to thrust, slowly, patiently. Callie moaned softly at first, and then with greater urgency, her fingers opening and closing on his back, her hips rising faster and faster against him.

She cried out suddenly, her thighs, her very essence gripping him, and then Mase felt the explosion shuddering through his entire body, too, a seizure of pure pleasure.

He collapsed against her, spent, whispering words of wonder and content in her ear. And she murmured against him, too, their bodies fitting together as if made for this sole purpose. He hadn't known it would be possible to feel this way again, Mase realized. And somehow, it was even more beautiful than he could have dreamed.

They made love again that afternoon, Callie playfully urging him to heights he had never experienced. She had a touch, a way—the same touch she had with her animals—that made him wild for her, obedient and daring and crazy to know her again, to possess her as she did him.

Callie made love with her whole being, as if every cell burst with heat and passion. She was never still, never quiet, every inch of her, even her soul, engaged in their joining. And she set him on fire.

When finally they heard the laughter of the returning children, they dressed hurriedly and scampered like kids themselves down the ladder. Callie pulled hay from his hair and he did the same for her. They both laughed.

"Like this is going to really fool someone," Callie teased as she brushed the hay from his shirt and the seat of his pants.

He quickly spun her around and did the same. "I feel like I've just been caught with my hands in the cookie jar," he said, and they both laughed again.

"I'll go first," Callie offered. "No one will notice."

"Go ahead," Mase said. "I'll walk over to the house in a few minutes. Tell Joey I'm showering or something."

"Okay," she replied, and turned to go.

He caught her, though. Pulled her back around and kissed her deeply before releasing her. Once he was alone in the barn with the horses, nickering and stirring at their feed buckets, he leaned against the wall and let out a deep breath. *"Wow."* He'd never fully believed in magic before. But now he knew how very real it was. Callie's magic had worked on him, too.

CHAPTER FOURTEEN

THE STORM BLEW DOWN from the Continental Divide that night. A hundred miles to the west, the mountains were shrouded in dense clouds. And, boy, did it rain at Someday Ranch. A bone-chilling downpour borne on high winds that rattled the windows and gates and shook the roof on the barn, spooking the horses.

Callie barely slept through the storm. Twice she went out in the middle of the night to check the animals and quiet them. But it wasn't the storm that kept her sleepless, it was the crazy, overwhelming love tormenting her.

She got up a little late, having finally dozed off toward morning. She showered, did her hair, even put on makeup. The whole time she fussed she was smiling—that secret, contented smile of a woman who has just been fulfilled beyond her wildest dreams.

Every moment she'd spent in Mase's arms was seared into her memory. Every touch and caress had branded her. No more losers for Callie Thorne. No other man could ever make her feel so wonderful, so beautiful and so satisfied. Mase was the one. Finally. And his secret barely mattered anymore. How bad could it be? He loved her, she dared to think. He had to love her.

She skipped down the stairs to the kitchen, trying to wipe the telltale grin off her lips, but she knew everyone would see it. Heck, she was glowing from head to toe. Who cared? They had all been playing matchmaker, anyway.

Mase was already gone, running errands with Tom, she learned from her mom. A dart of disappointment shot through her, but it was a small one. He'd be back. And they'd get together again. Maybe not in the barn—Callie almost giggled aloud—but his room wasn't far from hers. There was tonight. And a thousand more nights.

Callie's thoughts skidded to a halt, and she set down the jug of milk she was holding. A thousand nights? Mase lived in Denver.... Well, darn, she'd simply talk him into quitting his job, moving here. Maybe Sheriff Hatcher had a spot for him. *Sure.* She smiled again.

"You really are frisky this morning," Sylvia said when she walked in with Joey and Rebecca.

Callie gave the kids both a big hug. "I feel pretty good," she said matter-of-factly. "And how are you two little cherubs today?"

"I'm fine," Joey said, reaching for a cereal bowl from the dish rack.

"Me, too," Rebecca echoed, choosing a bowl for herself.

"Where are your parents?" Callie asked the little girl, still not quite believing the sound of Rebecca's voice.

"They went home."

"They'll be back later," Sylvia explained, and she got the two little ones seated with their breakfasts.

Jarod gave the therapy sessions that morning, and Callie offered to run into town to the feed store when Liz remembered she'd forgotten to tell Tom they were going to run out of rolled oats.

"I'll go," Callie said, and she wondered if she'd bump into Mase. Every cell in her body craved the sight of him, and she thought again that she'd convince Mase to leave Denver. He had to realize by now what a better life this was for him and Joey. Okay, so asking him to give up his life as a cop in Denver was a lot. But, jeez, she mused, love could conquer all.

She got the keys to the pickup and went out to start it. She had to turn on the wipers to clear the rain off the windshield. The sun was back out now, but the drive, the ditches, everything was muddy.

She revved the engine and put the gearshift in reverse. Suddenly, one of her visions came to her.

She was walking down the aisle, her dad at her side. The church was filled, and her gorgeous white dress trailed behind her. Rebecca was holding the train off the floor, and Joey was there, too, next to Rebecca. The smiling faces of her friends and family were all turned to watch her progress.

There was Mase, waiting at the altar. Her breath caught. He was so handsome, so delicious-looking in his tails and formal white shirt. Flowers surrounded him, and there were a few sniffles from the front rows—his mother on one side weeping joyously, Liz on the other side, a hankie in hand. The minister was smiling. It was a match made in heaven.

Callie blinked, but the vision kept on playing itself out.

"I do," she said.

"I do," he said.

He was pulling back her lacy veil, his lips meeting hers. She was only vaguely aware of the cheers and applause. Then they were walking back up the aisle, his ring on her finger, hers on his, all new and shiny....

A sudden rap at her car window startled Callie right out of her fantasy.

Francine. "Oh, I'm glad I caught you. If you're going to the store, grab me another gallon of milk."

"I will," Callie told her, "but you just ruined my wedding."

"Huh?" Francine said, but Callie was driving off.

The ranch road had taken a real beating during the night. It was a veritable washboard. Of course, Callie mused as she steered around the water-filled potholes, there'd been a ton of traffic on it, anyway, from the gymkhana. Subconsciously she noticed a set of peculiar tire tracks left in the mud, tracks leading off along an abandoned county road that crossed a portion of the Thornes' ranch then wound up into the hills. She really didn't register the tracks at all—not then—but drove straight past them, whistling to herself, images of Mase in the hay filling her head to overflowing.

She never ran into Mase and her dad. Not at the feed store and not on the highway. And certainly not at the grocery store. Her dad hated grocery shopping. But she did run into a dozen people from town who all wanted to stop and thank her for the great camp out. Callie had to agree. It had been wonderful. Nothing like the day after, though. Nothing like the hayloft...

Donna Knudson stopped her in the dairy section. Reese Hatcher's dispatcher was picking up coffee and cream for the coffeemaker in the sheriff's office. She, too, went on about the super weekend and how she'd caught a rainbow trout in the stream. "My very first. Can you believe it?"

"Bet you didn't clean it yourself," Callie said, reaching for two half gallons of milk.

"Well, no," Donna said, her hand flopping at the

wrist, a habit she had when she was talking. "My husband did the honors."

"Good for him," Callie said. "Well, gotta get going."

Then Donna leaned close and placed a hand on Callie's arm. "That Mase LeBow sure is a keeper, honey," Donna said conspiratorially. "I mean, bidding on a total stranger at the auction and getting the coolest guy there. Go figure."

Callie laughed. "He *is* nice. Did you meet him at the gymkhana?" she asked.

"Oh, my, no," Donna said, then she made that hand gesture again. "I met him the first time he stopped to talk to Reese at the office."

"Mase stopped at the sheriff's?"

"Oh, yes. And I think it's so neat, his hiding up here in our little town and all. And you guys, your whole family, that is, taking care of his boy like you are." Donna winked.

Hiding up here...? Callie frowned. She posed her next question carefully. "Mase told Reese Hatcher everything?" she asked.

"Well, sure, they're both in law enforcement, you know."

Callie's mind was whirling. Mase hiding Joey? From what? That trial. It had something to do with the trial. Something dangerous. Suddenly Mase was an open book. *Joey* was in danger, and he was using the Someday Ranch as a hideout, and... My God.

"You never know what'll happen when you buy a man, do you?" Donna was saying.

"No, you sure don't."

"And, I must admit," Donna continued, "I was as

surprised as Reese when Mase just up and quit his job last week.''

"He...quit?"

Donna drew in a breath. "But I...I thought you must have known. Oh, gosh, oh, my, no one said anything about keeping this a secret. Oh, goodness, I mean, the door to Reese's office was open, and he usually closes it if it's personal. Oh, I am sorry, Callie, I didn't..."

How Callie got out of there, through the checkout and into her truck, she never remembered. Her head felt as if someone had just dealt it a blow with a sledgehammer. The thoughts dashed across a black screen behind her eyes: some kind of threat to Joey's life; Mase at the bachelor auction; Mase with his son, looking downright menacing.

"Of course, of course," Callie moaned as she pulled out of the parking lot and onto the Shoshone Highway. *"Of course."*

Then she'd babbled away about her ranch being isolated, and he'd jumped at it. She could see the lightbulb that must have switched on in his head. And she'd thought fate had brought the two of them together. *Fate.* Oh, what a sucker she was.

No wonder he'd wanted Joey to stay at the ranch. And then—dumb, dumb, dumb—she'd shown up in Denver for her shopping trip *with* Joey. Mase's furious reaction... Now it all made sense.

Oh, Lord, Callie realized, he'd quit his job. Donna had told her Mase had quit. Why? It must have happened right before the gymkhana. What had he said? A vacation? She couldn't remember now.

"I knew it, I knew it," she whispered between clenched teeth as she sped along the open road. "I knew there was something terribly wrong."

She felt as if she'd been socked in the jaw. Anger, pain, anger again. He'd used her. Boy, had he ever used her. Even when she'd suspected something was wrong, he hadn't trusted her enough to confide in her.

Mase didn't trust her.

Yesterday. Oh, my God. The hayloft.

Tears rolled down her cheeks, and angrily she wiped them away. How could he have hurt her like this? If he had only told her, confided in her, even a hint…

She turned onto the ranch road, again passing those tire tracks but still not registering their significance. Instead, she was drilled to the core by sudden fear—Mase and Joey were in danger. Then the fear subsided and rage burned in her again. Then pain. As if she'd been mortally wounded.

By the time she spotted her dad's truck parked next to the barn, Callie's emotions were in a wild tangle. She didn't care, though. She only knew Mase LeBow was about to get it, and get it real good.

She got out of the truck, slammed the door and strode right up to Mase and her dad.

"Uh-oh," Tom said, loud enough for her to catch. "I've seen that face before." Then he not-so-discreetly disappeared around the corner of the barn.

She was vaguely aware of Jarod over in the ring, and Rebecca riding Kahlua, but she didn't care who saw or overheard.

"You son of a…" she began, turning her face up to Mase's. "I just found out everything. How…how *could* you do this?"

He said absolutely nothing. He just stared down at her, his eyes unreadable.

"Don't you dare pull a silent act on me, mister. I want to know what on earth was in your head when you lied to us. When you *used* us. And how about yesterday? How about *that?*"

Still he said nothing, but she could see an emotion flickering in his eyes now. Regret? *Ha,* she thought. "Don't you trust me even the littlest bit? Don't you know how much this hurts? You quit your job and don't even tell me?"

"Your father knows," he said after a moment.

"Oh, good, great, *Dad* knows. That makes it all hunky-dory. And Joey. There's a threat to Joey's life and you keep that a secret, too?"

"Look, Callie," Mase began, and he thrust a hand through his hair. "I was wrong. Dead wrong."

"Oh, my Lord," she said tartly, "you were wrong. Sure, now that the cat's out of the bag. Are you kidding me?"

"Okay, okay," he said, barely meeting her eyes, "I screwed up. I just thought…"

"You screwed something else, too," she said in a harsh whisper. "Literally."

There was nothing Mase could say to that, and he didn't even try.

"I can forgive you everything," Callie said, tears hot behind her eyes, "but Joey. Didn't you realize I needed to know about the threat to him? Do you think I would have made that trip to Denver and gone shopping? *Shopping?*"

"Of course not," he said under his breath.

"Well, when *were* you planning on telling me?"

"I…I was going to tell you before I leave to testify."

"Really."

"Yeah, Callie, really. Tonight. In the morning. I was going to have Reese stop out, and I thought I'd sit down with you and your folks and talk it over. Obviously," he said, his brows knitting, "I left it a little too long."

"You could say that."

"Look, Callie," he said, trying to explain, "I blew it. Okay? I did a stupid cop thing and played my cards too close to my chest. I didn't even let my own partner know what was going on. I thought the fewer who knew, the better."

She glared at him. "Why did you quit?"

"The police force?"

"Yes, of course. Why did you quit your job?"

He told her. All about the note he found under his door, his confrontation with Metcalf, the ensuing visit from his boss. "Hey," he said, "I knew the minute I quit it was the right thing to do. I was fed up with the city, the endless crime, the whole stinking thing."

"You never said that to me."

"Subject never came up."

"It would seem that no subject ever came up between us, Mase, except sex. That sure came up."

"It wasn't sex," Mase said tightly. "You can't believe that. I made mistakes, okay, but what we... shared, Callie, was not just sex."

"Whatever," she said loftily, disbelieving. Guys would say anything when put on the hot seat. Oh, you bet they would. And Mase was cut from the same cookie cutter. What a chump she'd been.

Still, Callie realized as she glared at him, the issue, the vital issue here, was Joey. Not her wounded pride or his male ego or any of it. Joey's safety was what really counted.

"Who's doing this?" she asked. "Who's threatening Joey?"

"I'm convinced the man behind it all is Richard Metcalf, but he's hired a guy we call the Hitman. He's the one actually searching for Joey. He's the one who's already committed murder. And it's his neck on the line, too, if I testify."

"But the cops haven't caught him," she pointed out.

"If I change my story, he's safe. No more arrest warrant, nothing. And Richard Metcalf is safe, too. You better believe Metcalf is footing the bills to keep me silent."

"Why not...kill you?" *Oh, God,* she thought.

"Can't get away with killing a cop. Not for long."

"So...so he threatened Joey," she said, and Mase nodded again. Abruptly, Callie's eyes widened. "You can't testify," she said with authority. "Absolutely not."

But he only laughed humorlessly. "You bet your life I'm going to testify. I'm going to nail those creeps to the wall."

Callie was aghast. "But...but Joey. Jocy..."

"Joey is just fine here. He's perfectly safe. Other than my old boss and Reese Hatcher, no one knows he's here. Not even my own parents know."

"But...oh, Lordy, what if I was followed when I left Denver with Joey that morning? What if...?"

"You weren't," Mase said with conviction. "Callie, I followed you myself for damn near fifty miles, and no one was on your tail."

"You...you're sure?"

"Yes, Callie, I'm sure."

By dinner everyone who needed to know about Mase's predicament had been told. It amazed Callie that they all believed he was doing the right thing by testifying. They even patted him on the back. He was a hero. Even more amazing to her was that no one faulted him in the least for keeping his troubles secret. Everyone seemed to understand.

Everyone but her.

She found Mase on the porch after dinner, which she'd skipped, complaining of a headache. It hurt so terribly to be close to him, her heart beating miserably, her soul still craving him despite his treachery. She had to talk to him, though. She couldn't let him go without trying one last time to talk some sense into him.

They stood face-to-face in the gathering darkness, and Callie steeled herself against the heady effect. "Don't testify," she begged. "For Joey's sake, don't do it, Mase."

"Callie," he said, and his voice was a caress to her ears, "don't you see? I could never live with myself if I ran from this."

"But…"

He reached out and put a silencing finger against her lips. "What kind of an example would I be for Joey if I gave in to my fears?"

She couldn't move. His hand was on her chin now, tilting it up, and when he spoke, the tone of his voice was soft, intimate.

"Everything will be okay," he said, and he smiled a little.

Callie stiffened and swatted his hand away. "Oh, you almost had me there," she said. "You just about had me, LeBow. But I'm not fooled for long. You know what you are?"

Mase sighed. "No. But I bet you're going to tell me."

"Darn tootin'," she said hotly. "You, Mase LeBow,

are just like every guy I've ever met. A loser.'' With that, Callie turned on her heel and stomped away.

MASE CROSSED THE WYOMING state line and drove into Colorado, trying to keep his mind on the upcoming ordeal on the witness stand. He'd been prepped thoroughly by the D.A. in Denver, gone over and over his testimony for months in mock sessions. And the D.A. himself had posed dozens of questions that Sleazebag, Metcalf's attorney, was no doubt going to ask in cross-examination. The D.A. felt they'd covered all the bases, though Mase was betting the man had to be rattled right now that his star witness had quit the police force. Sleazebag had to know, also, and he'd somehow use the knowledge in his cross-examination.

Mase steered along the interstate, following the jutting line of foothills to the west, and planned his answers to the inevitable questions.

"So, Detective LeBow," Sleazebag would say, "or should I call you *Mr.* LeBow, now that you've left the department?"

"Mr. LeBow will do, sir," Mase would answer, oh-so-polite, unruffled.

Then the attorney would, of course, ask why Mase had quit. The D.A. would leap to his feet, object on the grounds of irrelevancy, but the judge would allow the question. Heck, Mase had been in enough courtrooms during his years as a homicide detective to know the drill by heart.

What would he answer? The truth, naturally. He'd tell it exactly like it was, that he was fed up. Maybe he'd even get in a shot at Metcalf. "It's the rich crooks like Richard Metcalf, thinking they can get away with murder, who were the final straw."

Sleazebag would go ape, but it would be too late. The jury would have heard. And how could they not agree?

Mase tried to map it all out as he passed Fort Collins and headed south toward Denver.

He forced his mind to stay on the issue at hand, and yet Callie was always there, lurking in the shadowed corners of his brain. It was as if she'd always been there. Ever since he'd first laid eyes on her at the auction. Was that possible? Love at first sight?

Did he love her?

Mase didn't know. He loved everything about her. There was no denying that. And there was no denying the way they'd fit together in that hayloft. But he'd blown it. He sure as hell had made one big mess of their relationship.

He tried hard to recall the expressions on Callie's face the last time he'd seen her. Wounded. Disappointed. Worried. He saw Joey, too, holding Callie's hand out in the drive. His son wasn't stupid, and he'd been pouting a little, no doubt sensing the strain between his father and his new friend Callie. Two people the child...loved. But everyone else had been upbeat, wishing Mase luck, telling him to hurry back, as if the Someday Ranch were his home now.

It felt like home. Everything about the place, including Callie, was good for him. And yet he'd taken everyone's trust, used everyone, and betrayed them all. The curious thing was that no one blamed him. No one but Callie. And there was not a damn thing he could do to remedy that.

He got off I-25 on University in Denver and headed toward his house. If all went as planned, he might be called to the witness stand as early as tomorrow. The jury had been selected last week. The attorneys would make their opening statements, and then the D.A. would call Mase to the stand. That was the plan, anyway. Mase had been told he could be on the stand for one to two days. It was a critical time for Joey. But once Mase was done testifying, the danger would be over.

He could hardly wait. A couple of days.

Joey was safe, though, in good hands, well hidden from those creeps. It was all going to work out. And soon—three days, four?—Mase would be driving back to the ranch to get Joey.

And then what? He was jobless. But worse, far worse, he'd lost Callie. The best damn thing that had happened to him since Amy's death, and he'd single-handedly screwed it up.

He pulled into his drive, turned the car off and stretched. One day at a time, Mase told himself, take each day as it comes.

And maybe, just maybe, there was a little magic left for him at the Someday Ranch.

Hey, he could always hope, couldn't he?

CALLIE SAT BOLT UPRIGHT in the middle of the night, her pajamas soaked, her breath shallow, and she saw them as clear as day—the tire tracks. Those curious tire tracks in the mud on the abandoned county road. Tracks that never should have been there. And, she suddenly realized, a knife of fear plunging into her heart, they'd been made in the mud *after* the gymkhana was long over. Who had made them? And why on earth was she so darn scared?

Joey, she thought suddenly. Did it have something to do with Joey?

She rushed to the window, pulled open the curtain and stared at the bunkhouses. All was quiet.

It's okay, she told herself, *Joey is fine.*

Besides, Sylvia was sleeping next door to him. And Hal and Jarod and James were in the next room. Everything was perfectly all right, she thought. So why was her heart still beating furiously?

CHAPTER FIFTEEN

IT WAS SYLVIA WHO discovered that Joey was gone. At 7:00 a.m. she stood in the bunkhouse, hands on hips, and grumbled out loud. "Darn kid. He knows he's not supposed to leave here till I come to get him up. Rules are rules and they've got to be obeyed."

She did the obvious thing then, went next door to the girls' quarters and checked Rebecca's room.

"Have you seen Joey this morning?" she asked Rebecca, who was still in bed, rubbing her sleepy eyes.

But the little girl only shook her tousled head.

"Well, you get on up now, honey," Sylvia said, "and don't forget to brush your teeth. I'll be back in a minute."

Sylvia searched the rest of the girls' bunkhouse, poking her head in Marianne's room, then Linda's, but no one had seen the little boy. She was getting more annoyed by the second. Plus it was raining out. He'd better not be with the horses, she thought as she fetched a jacket from her own room. Most likely, though, he'd gone to the main house, breakfast on his mind.

She tromped through the rain and across the muddy yard to the house, talking to herself the whole way, and entered through the kitchen door. "Joey? You little devil. You in here?"

Callie had just come down the stairs when she heard

Sylvia's voice. "Did I hear you calling for Joey?" she asked as she entered the kitchen.

"I sure as blazes am," Sylvia said. "He just up and disappeared...."

"That's not at all like Joey," Callie said, "and in this rain." She cocked her head, meeting Sylvia's gaze, and a moment of uncertainty passed between the two women.

"You don't suppose he went out to see the horses...?" Sylvia began.

But Callie was no longer listening. It was as if an icy hand had just squeezed her heart. "Oh, no," she breathed. "Oh, my God."

By eight the place was a madhouse. Everyone was out in the cold, slashing rain searching for Joey, calling his name, checking every nook and cranny in the house, the barn, the bunkhouses, the riding ring, everywhere. Callie searched as hard as anyone, but in her heart she knew: Joey had been kidnapped.

At nine Tom telephoned Reese Hatcher, who said he'd be there in fifteen minutes. And then it was Callie's job to call Mase. It was the hardest call she'd ever made. "Oh, Mom," she whispered to Liz, who was sitting next to her on the edge of the couch, "what am I going to say to him?"

But Liz could only shake her head. There were no right words for a time like this.

Callie dialed his beeper, her fingers numb and shaking. He'd see the number of the ranch and call back immediately. She closed her eyes and tried to picture him. Was he at the courthouse already? On his way there? How long before he could get to a phone? Or maybe he was carrying his pager with him.

What was she going to say?

They waited, still sitting on the edge of the couch. A minute passed. It seemed more like an hour. Her mind churned frantically, searching for some way to tell Mase his son was missing, but nothing came to her. At one point she spun around to Liz and cried, "Why didn't I have Joey sleep upstairs in a guest room? *Why?*"

Another minute dragged by.

It was nearly five minutes before the phone in her lap rang, and she nearly jumped out of her skin. "Oh, God," she sobbed, and she managed to press the talk button.

It was him.

"Callie…?" he began.

But she cut him off, the words tumbling out of her mouth. "Joey's gone. Mase, he's *gone.*"

There was a long pause, a lifetime of seconds dragging by, and she could feel his horror through the many miles that separated them. He finally spoke, but all he could say was "You're sure? He couldn't be…?"

"He's gone," Callie repeated, a whisper torn from her throat. She bit her lower lip and held back tears. Liz clutched her free hand.

Another moment of torturous silence followed. Then Mase breathed, "Berry. Hank Berry. It can't be anyone else."

"Oh, Mase," she cried, "how did he find Joey? How…"

"I don't know. God, I don't know. Have you called Hatcher?"

"Yes. He'll be here any minute. Oh, Mase, oh, Lord…"

"I know, I know. Just hold on, Callie. I'll be there as fast as I can. I'll fly up to Casper, rent a car. It will be okay," he said, but there was no conviction in the harsh rasp of his voice.

"I'm so sorry," she whispered.

"It's not you who should be sorry," he said painfully. "This is my fault." And then he hung up.

Reese was the one who found the note. It had been left next to Joey's bed, and no one had noticed. It was typed on plain white paper, and it read; "We will return the boy safely after the trial if your testimony is satisfactory."

Reese picked the note up by the corner and put it in a plastic bag. "This goes to the lab," he said in a gravelly voice.

Then they all sat in the living room while the sheriff asked dozens of questions. Questions and questions and more stupid police questions. They should be out looking for Joey. Something, Callie thought. Anything but sitting here.

She did remember to tell Reese about the peculiar tire tracks on the abandoned county road. She hadn't thought he would find much significance in her story, but surprisingly, he wanted to drive straight there.

"What are you thinking?" Tom asked the sheriff.

"It's like this," Hatcher said, finally putting away his notebook and rising, "there's one decent road out of here, the Shoshone Highway. Now, if it were *me* who snatched the boy, I sure wouldn't count on taking that road. How would I know someone wouldn't call the police, who'd put up a blockade before I could reach the interstate? Now, as I see it, this Hitman character, or whoever it is who's got Joey LeBow, he woulda scouted the area. If he's got a map, he's gonna see that old county road on it."

"But it's impassable," Tom said, frowning. "I'm

sure that up in the hills there's no way a vehicle is going to get through. Heck, last time I was that far along the thing, there were places where the old road-bed had literally fallen away into the canyon. I don't see how this man…''

But Hatcher put up a hand. "He don't know that, now, does he? Not unless he drove all of it, which I doubt.''

Callie cocked her head. "But the mud, Reese? No one in his right mind would try that road.''

"You wouldn't, Miss Callie, and Tom and I wouldn't be that dumb. But Mase told me this guy's a dude, a real city boy. And we all know they ain't got much sense. Now, let's go give it a look-see.''

Callie and Jarod rode with the sheriff, and Tom and Liz followed in the pickup truck. The whole way out, Reese talked on the radio, instructing Donna to call for a county-wide net to be set up. Then he radioed the state police and requested the same. He was assured every road in eastern Wyoming would be covered, and the state police would contact the Colorado highway patrol and put them on the alert, too. The photo of Hank Berry would be faxed to all police headquarters, though no one had a picture of Joey.

"When Mase gets here,'' Callie said, "he'll have one. In his wallet. Something.''

It occurred to her, as it must have occurred to every-one, that whoever had Joey could be miles and miles away by now. In Nebraska, for goodness' sake, or even Montana. She only prayed he wasn't too far, that maybe he hadn't taken Joey till just before dawn, when the dogs were still inside and Sylvia was dead to the world.

Stop it, Callie thought. None of it mattered now.

Joey was all that counted. Getting Mase's son back. Unharmed.

She pictured Mase. Alone, so alone right now. *Oh, Mase,* she thought, *hurry and get here. Hurry.*

She kept an image of Mase in her mind's eye. But she didn't dare try to envision Joey. She was too terrified of what she might see.

MASE HAD SPOKEN to Callie on his cell phone just as he'd been searching for a parking spot at the courthouse. His very first instinct was to control the fear and think everything out. His stomach twisting into a thousand knots, he sped home and grabbed a change of clothes—he was in his court garb of suit and tie. He also snatched up the extra cell phone battery, everything he could think up.

His gun. Two spare clips of ammo. And his badge. He'd never get on a flight without his police credentials.

Think, think, he commanded himself as he stood in his bedroom, his heart racing. Was he forgetting anything?

His folks. *Damn.* It ran through his head that he should call them, but he'd spoken to them just last night when he'd gotten in, and they didn't need to know about this. Not yet, anyway.

He used the cell phone while he drove and got a booking on a noon commuter flight to Casper. And then he went straight back to the courthouse, where the first person he found was the D.A. He gave Denver's number-one lawyer a thumbnail description of what had gone down.

"You go and find your son, Mase," the D.A. told him. "You can testify later. It doesn't matter. If there's anything I can do on this end, call in some federal help as soon as the law allows—anything—you just let me know.''

''Thanks,'' Mase muttered, distracted.

Then he located his boss, who began the litany of how Mase's job was still available and they all missed him and...

''They got Joey,'' Mase said tightly, and he had to go through the same spiel as he had with the D.A.

He was twitching with impatience by the time he got back outside into his car and raced toward the airport, and he had to keep wiping off the sweat that collected on his forehead.

Metcalf, he thought. Metcalf would realize that Mase wasn't testifying. Would he contact Berry and tell him to release Joey? Could it be that goddamn simple? No, he thought, no way, Metcalf wasn't going to contact Berry—if he even knew exactly where Berry had taken Joey. There was only one way Mase was going to find his son, and that was to do it himself. He pressed down the accelerator and clamped down on the fear that was rising in his throat.

Hold on, Joey. Hold on, son.

HANK BERRY HAD NEVER SPENT a more miserable day in his life. He stoked the half-rusted potbellied stove in the sheepherder's cabin and felt a shiver seize his limbs. He was freezing, tired from the long trek through the storm, and he was hopping mad. How in hell could they put a road on a state map when there was no road? At least nothing any sane man would call a road.

''Mister?'' came the kid's whiny voice. ''Mister, I'm wet.''

The Hitman shoved some more sticks he'd collected into the yawning mouth of the stove. All it did was smoke. "Yeah, well, kid," he said, "I'm just as goddamned wet as you. Think I like it?" He'd have told the kid his Gucci loafers were ruined, too, but hell, the boy wouldn't know a Gucci loafer from an Armani suit.

The brat peered around him and looked into the stove. "You put too many twigs in there," he said. "It's smothering the fire."

"Will you shut up? What are you, a Boy Scout or something?"

The kid subsided into a corner of the old, abandoned shack, shivering, hugging himself. The Hitman threw him a look of pure malevolence. *Stupid cop's kid.*

After an hour or so the stove finally began to give off a little heat. The Hitman cracked an already-broken chair over his knee and shoved the splintered pieces into the pitiful fire. He didn't shove in too many, though, 'cause maybe the kid was right about smothering that puny flame.

The worst part about his car sliding off the road— other than having to march through the storm for God knows how many miles—was that he was out of communication with Metcalf. Out of communication with the world. Out of warm, dry clothes, out of food and water, and pretty much out of luck.

It was still daylight, though. He spread out the map on the dusty, tilted table and tried to figure out where they were. How many miles had they walked? And in what direction? For all he knew, just over that next ridge might be a road or even a town. But he couldn't very well hitchhike with the kid, now, could he? Every law enforcement agency in the state was on the lookout for him. He was in a real fix. And he was beginning to wonder if there was any way out of it.

The sheepherder's cabin was tiny. Maybe only twelve feet by twelve feet. When the kid moved to the fire, he had to edge around Hank.

"'Scuse me," the kid said.

The Hitman made a grumbling sound.

What was he going to do with him? The plan had been to drive back to Denver via the western corner of Nebraska. Both he and Metcalf had figured that by the time he reached Denver, the cop would already have testified that he hadn't seen anything, and the Hitman would let the kid off on a street corner with a quarter to call the cops.

But now... What *was* he going to do? Until he talked to Metcalf and got the okay to let the kid go, he was stuck. Stuck, lost in the wilderness and starving to death. It was a helluva mess. And outside, the storm just kept moving across the high prairie. It looked as if it could go on for days. *Great.*

The kid finally took a nap on the broken cot, and the Hitman stared at him. He could leave him right here. The trouble was, if anything happened to the kid, LeBow would never stop searching for him, not to mention the fact that every other cop in the nation would be looking, too.

Right now the money Metcalf was paying him wasn't half enough.

The kid woke up sometime that afternoon and blinked sleepy eyes, not quite sure for a minute where he was. Then he looked as if he were going to cry.

"You start whining," Hank said, "and I swear I'll...I'll give you a spanking you won't forget, kid." He glared at him.

That worked for a while, but then the kid started pouting. "I'm really hungry, mister," he said in a small voice.

"So? You think I'm not? You're so smart, why don't you figure out how we're going to eat. Huh?"

"You'd tell Callie," the boy said then, reluctantly.

"What?"

"That I've got—" the kid reached into his jacket pocket "—these." He produced a bag of M&M's. "You won't tell Callie, will you?"

The Hitman's eyes widened. "Where did you get those, kid?"

"Francine gave them to me, but I'm not supposed to tell Callie."

"Well, hell, kid," Hank said, "I can keep a secret." He felt his stomach growl in anticipation.

Joey was smiling, a little smile that lit up his whole face. He tore open the bag and the Hitman held his hand out. "Red are my favorites," Joey said. "What're yours?"

Hank took a few from the boy's hand and said, "Hey, red are my favorite, too." He didn't know it, but he was smiling right back at Joey LeBow.

CHAPTER SIXTEEN

MASE HARDLY REMEMBERED the flight to Casper or the drive to the ranch in the rental car. All he knew was crushing fear and overpowering impatience.

He drove up the familiar ranch road under pewter-gray skies. There was a stiff wind blowing, and the ranch looked entirely different, bleak, the color washed from the countryside, the horses standing rumps to the storm, heads hanging dispiritedly. As if they knew.

He got out of the car and started up the walk to the house, but before he could raise a hand to knock, the door opened and Tom Thorne stood there, his face a study in solemnity.

"You got here fast," he said.

"Any news?" Mase asked tersely.

"There was a note. Reese found it, and he's going to get it checked out."

"What'd it say?"

"That they'll return Joey safely after the trial if you say the right thing."

Mase swore. "Anything else?"

Tom shook his head.

He hadn't expected any more, but still, his gut twisted at the evidence of their helplessness.

Walking into the living room, he saw that everyone was gathered there, all those familiar faces. But they, too, were tainted with fear and anxiety.

"What's being done?" Mase began.

"Sheriff Hatcher's called the state patrol and the Casper police. He's got an APB out on that man," Tom said.

"Hank Berry."

"That's the one."

He heard Callie's voice before he saw her. She was coming from the kitchen, saying, "Has Mase...?" When she saw him, she stopped short, then she rushed to him and he took her into his arms.

"Oh, Mase, oh, I'm so, so sorry," she cried, and he held her and stroked her hair, unaware of the audience, aware only of the pain they were all sharing.

With some effort he disengaged himself and held her at arm's length. "It'll be all right," he said with a lot more confidence than he felt. "We'll find Joey."

Mase forced aside his own fears and sat with the group—all business now, the cop again. He asked the same questions as Reese Hatcher had that morning, but added a few of his own. Were there footprints found outside the bunkhouse, a broken window, car or foot tracks leading anywhere? What time had the storm begun? Had the dogs barked?

"Stupid dogs hide when there's a bad storm," Liz told him. "If it hadn't been raining so hard..."

"It's okay," Mase said, "just bad luck. No one's to blame. I'm the one who underestimated Hank Berry." Then he looked at Callie. "Tell me about those tire tracks you saw," he said, and she told him everything she knew, including Reese Hatcher's theory that Berry had driven down the old county road for a few miles, scouting it as an escape route.

"Someone is checking it out?" Mase asked, but he saw a lot of eyes drop.

Tom Thorne spoke up first. "The road is most likely impassable. Especially after this storm."

"What about checking it by helicopter?" Mase began, but as soon as he'd spoken, he realized that was impossible in such a storm.

"Too much wind in the canyons up there," Tom said in corroboration.

"So how *do* we check it out?" Mase asked.

Callie cleared her throat. "On horseback. But not till first light."

"First light!" Mase was aghast. "That's crazy." He shook his head. "No," he objected, "there has to be another way."

But in the end there wasn't. The search along the old road was going to have to wait till dawn. Hours and hours and hours away.

They spent the evening touching base with every law enforcement agency in the state. Reese came by twice. And it was Mase and Jarod who discovered the tracking device Hank Berry had placed on the underside of Callie's pickup.

Mase dropped it into a plastic evidence bag, his jaw locked. He should have known, should have checked, should have guessed. Should have, should have… *Easy to say now,* he thought, furious with himself.

On the porch, the storm still swirling around them, Callie laid a gentle hand on his arm. "You took every precaution, Mase," she said softly. "Please don't keep blaming yourself."

"Goddamn it, I screwed up. Can't you see that? Can't you accept the truth?"

"Mase…"

"No," he said in a hard voice. "If I'd have trusted

you, you and your parents and everyone else, maybe…
Hell, Joey would be fine right now.''

''Anger isn't going to help.''

But he only laughed without humor. ''It beats being scared, Callie.''

THE NEXT MORNING they were up before dawn. Mase wondered if anyone had slept; they all looked haggard.

Francine had breakfast ready and bag lunches for those who would be out searching for Joey, lots of hot coffee and trays of food ready to feed any deputies or townsfolk or state troopers who might stop by.

Sylvia was going to man the phones—a cordless that she carried around in her pocket and a cell phone. She was Communications Central, she said. The Browns, Rebecca's parents, had returned and were helping with the kids and everyday chores that had to be done.

Reese Hatcher came by at seven and sat hunched over Forest Service topographical maps spread out on the dining room table.

Mase stood at a window, every nerve in his body jumping with impatience. It was still raining out, vertical lines of rain that stitched the gray sky to the earth. A scene that accurately reflected the misery filling him. *Joey,* he thought, *I'm coming. Hang in there, son.*

A thousand times he'd pictured Berry's cadaverous face looming over Joey, doing unspeakable things, torturing him. Then reason would reassert itself, and Mase would remember that Joey had been taken hostage to assure Mase didn't testify. He had to believe Joey was safe or he'd go out of his mind.

Callie was already in the barn saddling horses, gathering slickers.

Sheriff Hatcher finally stood up and hitched his belt.

"Okay, this is how we'll do it. I got my men still out scouring the roads, everyone statewide is still on alert. Tom, Liz and Marianne have volunteered to cover all the ranch roads in a truck. Me and Jarod will cover the neighboring ranch roads in my Blazer. Mase and Callie are taking horses to follow the county road. And Peter insists on going with them." Hatcher eyed Peter. "It's gonna be rough goin', son."

"I know," the twelve-year-old said, "but I have to go. Callie and I already talked about it."

Mase fixed Peter with a hard gaze. "You, my boy, are staying here."

Peter began to argue, but just then Callie dashed in to announce the horses were saddled and ready, and he was too impatient and too worried to argue with both of them. He let it drop.

All three were dressed warmly when they left the house—down vests, waterproof gloves and boots. Long slickers awaited them in the barn. They had full saddlebags: food, water, grain for the horses, extra rain gear. First-aid kits. With Beavis and Butt-Head running alongside the horses, they headed across the fields on a diagonal to join up with the dirt road. It was cold and wet, although the rain had quit for a time, and the roadway was slippery. It was slow going, the horses laboring upward, their sleek hides wet with a mixture of sweat and rain.

Mase felt his skin chafing against the saddle, and he was tempted to get off and walk, but he was afraid he'd hold them up.

"You okay?" Callie asked more than once, seeing him shift his position.

"I'm fine," he said, tight-lipped.

They went on, the land rising. The road was barely

passable, and Mase kept an eye out for tire tracks, but the rain had washed away any sign of a vehicle's passage.

"Do you really think he could have driven this?" Mase asked.

"So far, sure. It'd be slow, but the road's intact. And yesterday it didn't rain as much, so the road wasn't as muddy. He could have made it."

"He might not have taken this road at all," Mase said quietly. "We could be on a wild-goose chase."

"We're not the only ones looking," Callie reminded him. "Someone will spot him."

By late morning the sun was breaking through the clouds, and the puddles sparkled in the brightness. They stopped for lunch by a stream, where they watered the horses, loosened their girths and let them graze a bit.

Mase couldn't bear the halt. He couldn't eat, couldn't sit down. He paced, studying the ground for tracks, unfolding the map Hatcher had given him, trying to pinpoint their location.

"You mean we're only this far?" he asked when Callie consulted the map.

"We're close to the top, then it starts descending toward the highway. Will you sit down and eat something, Mase?"

"No," he said. "My butt's too sore, anyway."

"These sandwiches are good, Mase," Peter said. "You should try one. Francine makes good sandwiches, you know? Here, you want to try mine?"

"No, thanks," Mase said.

Callie looked at Peter, raised her eyebrows and shrugged. She did, however, protest when Mase tried to feed his lunch to the dogs.

Peter started acting strangely when they got under way again. Mase only noticed when he heard the sharp note of alarm in Callie's voice.

"Peter," she said. "Peter? Why are you stopping?"

Mase turned and saw that Peter had reined in his horse and was sitting there, his head hanging between his shoulders.

"Peter, honey, are you okay?" Callie rode back to where the boy was sitting so still. "Peter?"

Mase turned his horse, impatient. *Never should have let the kid tag along,* he was thinking, when Peter sat bolt upright.

"I see it!" he yelled, his voice shrill with excitement.

"What? What do you see, Peter?"

Peter cocked his head. "The black car. Joey in the black car," he said, and he blinked and pointed ahead.

Mase had never believed in the kid's clairvoyant ability. But he did now. He had to. "Where?" he demanded, his heart racing.

"Up there. Up there ahead." Peter spurred his mount and led the way.

Mase looked at Callie, and she at him, but there was nothing either dared to say. They simply followed, hope springing in their breasts.

The rain returned with a vengeance before they'd gone far, and was accompanied by a bone-chilling wind. The horses hated walking into the storm; they had to be urged on, their instincts telling them to turn their backs to the elements. Cold water trickled down Mase's neck despite the slicker, and his hands ached as they gripped the reins.

He gave Callie a sidelong glance. Her hood was pulled tight around her face, a few strips of hair plastered wetly on her forehead. Her shoulders were hunched. They were all soaked, cold, miserable. And it was his fault. He closed his eyes, felt the rain stinging him, and told himself he deserved it. But Callie and Peter didn't.

They rounded a curve. The road snaked along ahead of them, a stream flowing beside it. The day had darkened with the rain, and the sky was low and oppressive, the horizon blotted out. Mase was starting to think that maybe they should give up, turn around. Nobody had driven up here with Joey. There was no car, no black car. Peter was just a hyper kid with a questionable imagination.

"There!" he heard Peter yell.

He raised his head and peered through the gloom. Peter was cantering ahead on his pony, and Callie galloped past him. Mase spurred his tired horse into a trot and felt his sore rear hit the saddle with a lurch. Then he saw it. A black car, streaked with mud, lying nearly on its side where the road fell away to the stream.

Callie had jumped off her horse and was running to the car. Peter was there, too. Mase jogged his mount up and got off stiffly. He tried to make his legs run, but he could only limp awkwardly.

"It's empty," Callie panted as he neared the car. "They're gone."

Mase checked the license plates. Colorado. He pulled open a door with difficulty because of the angle of the car and checked inside. No one, nothing but an empty soda can on the floor. He opened the glove compartment; the vehicle was a rental car, no papers giving the name of the renter. Nothing.

"This is it," Callie said, "isn't it? They got stuck, got out of the car and had to go on foot."

Mase backed out of the slanted front seat and stood there. "Maybe. Probably."

"I told you. Joey was in the car," Peter said.

"Where is he now, Peter?" Callie asked, desperation in her voice.

"I don't know," Peter told her, his voice subdued. "I can't see that far."

"I'm calling Sheriff Hatcher," Mase said. "He needs to know." He pulled the cell phone out of his pocket and dialed. It was a poor connection, but he got through to Donna in the Lightning Creek office and filled her in on what they'd found. "Tell the sheriff we're going on. They can't be far. If he can make it up the road, we're about eight miles past the ranch."

Mase clicked off the phone and stood there in the gray, relentless rain wondering how, in all this immensity, they would ever find Joey.

Reason told him Berry would have stayed on the road, and since they hadn't passed him and Joey on the way in, Mase figured they should just keep going.

They rode on into the storm along the badly rutted road. The rain was letting up a little, Mase thought, but how long could they stay out here in this weather? What would happen when it got dark?

He peered up at the leaden sky so often his neck was getting stiff. Could a chopper make it in before nightfall? No way, he realized, not unless the conditions improved drastically.

"Whoa," he heard Callie say, and he saw her horse shy at something lying in the road. She reined in, then one of the dogs ran up to sniff at it. Whatever it was looked like a snake to Mase.

"What is it?" he asked.

"I don't know," she said, getting off her horse. She

bent down toward the object, and Mase heard her give a startled cry. She picked it up and held it, her eyes shining, a smile spreading on her glistening wet face.

"It's Joey's!" she said. "It's his belt."

"Let me see." She handed it to Mase. Yes, it was Joey's. Tooled leather, a cowboy belt given to him by his grandparents. He held it, the rain pounding on his head, a wet strip of leather in his hand, and he knew the first real stirrings of hope.

"That's Joey's, yup," Peter was saying. "I remember it. That's his."

"He left it for us," Callie said. "Somehow he got it off and dropped it. Oh, Mase, he's one smart kid."

Mase held on to the belt, his heart squeezing.

"Show it to the dogs," Callie said breathlessly. "Maybe they can follow the scent. Maybe. I mean, they're not tracking dogs, but they know Joey."

She took the belt and called the dogs over. They sniffed at the leather while Callie crouched in the mud, an arm around each dog's neck. "Find Joey," she coaxed. "Find Joey. This is his belt, you dumb mutts. Where is he? Where's Joey? Go on, find him."

They looked up at her with big brown eyes, their tails making circles in the air, their bodies quivering with excitement.

"Find Joey," she said again, and the dogs raced off along the road, noses to the ground.

"Oh, dear Lord," Callie breathed. "Oh my goodness."

Mase watched in amazement until the dogs disappeared around a bend in the road. "It's going to be okay," he dared to say aloud. "My God, Joey's all right." And for once, for just a heartbeat, he actually believed it.

CHAPTER SEVENTEEN

CALLIE WATCHED the change come over Mase as if she were in the throes of one of her fantasies. No longer was he the troubled father on a life and death quest— now he was a cop. Professional, emotionless. The menace she'd first seen at the bachelor auction was back in those cool blue eyes.

She could see the metamorphosis take place; she watched as he took his gun from his vest pocket, ejected the clip into his hand, checked it and rechambered it. Then, instead of putting the gun in his pocket, he shoved it into the waistband at the back of his jeans.

She shivered. "Do you think you'll…need that?"

But Mase didn't reply. Instead, he started to remount.

"Mase, what about the sheriff? Shouldn't you…" Callie began, but Mase was already moving, on the hunt.

It was Callie who used the cell phone to contact Reese and give him their location. Sheriff Hatcher covered in an hour and a half the territory it had taken them half the day to ride on horseback, and his vehicle paid the price. By the time he reached them, the Blazer was covered in mud halfway up the fenders and an acidic smoke was rising from beneath the hood.

Reese stuck his head out the mud-splattered window and said, "Caught up with the dogs yet?"

"Not yet," Mase said, "but they can't be far now."

Reese led the way in the Blazer and the rest of them followed on horseback. Within a mile they came across the dogs, waiting, their tails still going like propellers.

Callie rode up to them and they took off across a broad, grassy plain, away from the road. The rain had let up a bit, with the sudden lifting of clouds that occurred in the high country, but mist hung on the hillsides in eerie masses.

It was slow going across impossibly rough terrain. The horses skidded down the sides of gullies, then stumbled up the other side. Reese often had to drive around the gulches and meet them on the opposite side, taking up precious time. And the smoke leaking from under the hood was ominous.

Mase was impatient to the point of anger. Not that Callie blamed him. She herself was scared, tired and wet, and frantic for Joey. She didn't say much and kept busy watching the muddy trail, listening to the grinding of the Blazer and trying to keep Beavis and Butt-Head from running too far ahead. Reese and Mase were afraid the dogs would alert Joey's captor to their presence.

It began to rain again shortly after five. A cold drizzle that seeped out of a hazy sky and straight into her bones. She was worried about all of them, but especially concerned about Peter. He was awfully young to be undergoing this ordeal, although, if truth be told, Peter's excess energy was standing him in good stead.

It wasn't long before Mase pulled up his horse and dismounted. "I'm going to walk. Reese can ride my horse. That Blazer's holding us up."

She would have protested and insisted she walk, but he was already striding toward the smoking car, stepping over rocks and bunchgrass, his head down and his shoulders hunched.

"Okay, whatever," she said under her breath as she wondered if this wasn't the craziest thing she'd ever done. Shouldn't they use the cell phone, call for backup no matter how long it took? It was a futile notion, though, because any fool could see there was no stopping Mase. He'd walk till he dropped, and then he'd crawl. Reese gave her a look and then shook his head as he mounted Mase's horse and kicked it into a trot. He knew. They all knew this was crazy. Still, they stumbled on into the gathering dusk while the rain kept beating away at them.

The cabin emerged from the haze as if it were a camera trick, a refocusing of a lens by a skillful operator. Callie blinked, wondering if it was one of her fantasies.

Next to her, Reese reined in his horse and said softly, "Whoa there, boy," so she knew it must be real.

At the sheriff's words Mase looked up. He froze, and Callie saw that dark menace take hold of him. He slipped a hand under his vest, around to the small of his back. Just checking. Callie shivered.

The dogs almost gave them away. Both mutts started racing toward the cabin, and Callie had a devil of a time whistling them in. When they finally came back to her side, she snatched them both by their collars.

The mist was moving in patches across the plain, and for a moment the cabin came into clear view. Callie's heart stopped. There was smoke curling into the leaden sky from an old rusted stovepipe. Someone was in there.

"Sheepherder's cabin," Reese said next to her, and Mase turned and nodded. Then he pulled the gun out and clicked off the safety. Reese had his own weapon, the shotgun he'd brought along from the Blazer.

Oh, dear Lord, Callie thought, *this is real.*

"Peter and Callie, you stay here and hold the horses and those mutts," the sheriff said. "Don't move, don't come any closer to the cabin. You hear shots, just wait. You got that?"

Peter nodded, wide-eyed, and Callie muttered some kind of an assent. Her lips were trembling and her mouth was dry. What if somebody got hurt? What if somebody got... Oh, my God.

Mase was already moving toward the cabin, crouching. There was a tension to his movement that frightened Callie almost more than the gun in his hand. Sheriff Hatcher sent Callie one last warning look, then took off after Mase.

"Joey's inside," Peter whispered in a scared voice, his hands gripping the reins of all three horses.

"Is he all right?" Callie whispered back.

But Peter only shrugged.

MASE DIDN'T SHOW an iota of fear. But inside, in his head and his gut and his heart, he'd never been more afraid in his life.

He sensed Hatcher behind him now as they neared the side of the cabin, the side with no window. A thousand scenarios beat at his brain—the thousand things every cop knew could go wrong. He forced himself to put them aside, but it was hard. God, but it was hard. Joey, he kept thinking. It was his boy in there, his son, the only thing he had left.

He felt Hatcher touch his elbow as they stole up to the cabin wall. Mase knew what the touch meant—to hold up for a moment.

The rain was coming down again with a vengeance. That was good. The racket it would be making on the tin roof would cover them. If only he could see inside, see where Joey was, where Berry was.

He turned quietly, still crouching, and signaled that he was going to try to get a look inside. Hatcher frowned then nodded, and Mase slowly edged around the corner toward the window near the front door.

Mase wiped the rain from his eyes, then reclasped his gun in both hands, keeping it lowered. Slowly, carefully, he positioned himself so that he could get a quick glance through the dirty glass.

It took only a fraction of a second to look in and back off. He stood next to the window, still crouched, and let out a calming breath, assessing what he'd just seen: Berry poking something into a potbellied stove and a tiny figure curled up on a sagging cot—Joey.

Hatcher was next to him now, and Mase gave him a sidelong glance, then whispered, "Berry's at the stove, back to us, left-hand corner. Joey's on a cot, right side."

Hatcher nodded. "Okay," he whispered back, "you force the door, I'll take Berry out."

Mase returned his nod. He took a long breath, then met Hatcher's eyes. "On three," he whispered, his muscles tensing.

Hatcher nodded again.

Mase ducked beneath the window, then straightened in front of the door. Hatcher followed. Quietly, the sheriff pumped a shell into the chamber of the shotgun.

Mase took another breath and whispered, "One… two…"

...*THREE*. CALLIE COULD hear his voice in her head as she watched in dread, her heart bucking in her chest.

It was over in a few seconds. Mase broke down the door with one well-placed kick. Hatcher rushed in past him, shotgun raised, then Mase disappeared inside, too. Callie heard the sheriff thunder out his warning, there were a couple of yells, a thump loud enough to make her jump, and then utter silence.

She couldn't help it; she couldn't stop herself no matter what the sheriff or Mase had said. She told Peter to stay put, then sprinted across the muddy field to the open door of the cabin and burst inside, panting.

"Joey!" she cried, and flung herself on him. He sat huddled in a corner next to a cot, looking scared to death. But okay. He looked okay.

"For God's sake, Callie," she heard Mase growl angrily, and she glanced over to where he was holding his gun on a thin-faced man dressed incongruously in a muddy, rumpled suit. A man Sheriff Hatcher was handcuffing.

She hugged Joey, she laughed and cried, and finally she held him out at arm's length. "Oh, we were so worried, Joey."

"I'm okay," Joey said, "but I'm hungry. Me and him, we finished all the M&M's this morning."

"The...?" Callie began, but then she laughed and wept again as Mase strode over and gathered Joey into his arms, clutching him so tightly that Joey finally protested.

"I knew you'd come, Daddy," Joey said when Mase set him down. "I knew it."

Mase started to say something, but nothing came out, and Callie could tell he was holding in tears. She looked from Mase to Joey and back and felt her own tears start all over again.

IT WAS A LONG NIGHT, one that Callie would always remember. The state troopers and local deputies arrived in four-wheel drive vehicles with tire chains shortly after midnight. There was some confusion then, because Callie insisted she lead the horses out in the morning, and Mase argued that a trooper could do it. But she held firm, and in the end Reese stayed with her, and the cops transported Mase and the Hitman and the two boys out in the Jeeps. It was a quick leave-taking. Mase grumbled that Callie was being stubborn about the horses, and Reese took Callie's side. Then they were all climbing into the vehicles, headlights piercing the blackness on the high prairie.

Callie cried until the grinding of the departing engines was only a memory. Then she sat on the cot and sniffed, angry at herself for being such a wimp where Mase was concerned.

"Mase is an all-right guy," Reese growled, handing her a sandwich brought up by his men, "but he don't understand about horses."

Callie took the sandwich and devoured it. Reese was right. And she was awfully glad to have a skilled horseman with her to get the three animals back to the ranch. But watching Mase and Joey leave, with only quick, impersonal hugs... Well, it felt a lot like having her heart torn right out of her breast.

"Love," Reese reflected, eating away.

THEY WERE NEARLY BACK at the Someday Ranch by noon. Neither Callie nor Reese had gotten much sleep, and they'd left the cabin at six in the morning, a rare summer frost lying on the ground and tingeing the sagebrush silver in the first light of day.

They made excellent time despite their exhaustion, only stopping to water and rest the horses twice. Reese used his cell phone to keep everyone abreast of their progress and to check on the status of Hank Berry, who was being held in jail in Lightning Creek. The plan was for Reese to escort the Hitman to Denver within the next couple of days.

Callie did get to speak to Mase once, but only briefly, since the phone battery was low and Reese wanted to save it in case of an emergency. The words she spoke to Mase were trite: "Are you okay? Is Joey okay?"

To which Mase had replied, "You sure you don't want someone to ride up and meet you? God, Callie, you must be wiped out."

What she wanted to say was how much she missed them, how terribly relieved she was. Instead, they said a hasty goodbye.

She and Reese plodded along on the horses, taking turns ponying the third horse down the muddy road. At least it had stopped raining, and the sun was trying to break through the thick clouds that clung to the hillsides. It was a heartening sight. It seemed to Callie that the storm had brought nothing but misery to everyone. It was over, though, and she had to believe everything was going to be okay now. Even with Mase. Things had to work out. They *had* to.

They were greeted by the entire ranch and what seemed like half the community when they finally rode in. Everybody hugged Callie and had to hear the whole story of how Peter had "seen" Joey and the car and how Mase and Reese had gotten the drop on Berry at the cabin.

Callie ate a huge lunch, and with Joey and Rebecca sitting on either side of her, she related her version of the heroics of Mase and Reese and all the law enforcement troops who'd braved that dangerous drive up to the cabin.

"Of course," she said between bites, "the sheriff's Blazer is history."

"Aw, we'll get it towed down soon as the road dries," Reese said.

"Like next spring," Tom added, and everyone laughed.

Callie was acutely aware of Mase, who appeared in the door and stood quietly listening, his gaze on her. Oh, how desperately she wanted to be alone with him. There were so many questions, but the opportunity never arose. Not that afternoon or even the following morning. And then she heard from Sylvia—not from Mase—that he and Joey were leaving for Denver after lunch. Her heart stopped beating entirely. She'd known, of course, that they had to go. Mase still had to testify; the trial was in full swing. But somehow the news came as an awful blow. What was going to become of her and Mase?

It wasn't until Mase was heading toward the rental car that Callie finally got a few seconds alone with him. Her heart was bursting with a hundred, a thousand things she wanted to say, but all that came out was "Drive carefully, Mase. And, Joey, you be a good boy."

Mase's eyes met hers, and she saw something in their depths. A promise? A beginning? Or an end?

"We wouldn't have found Joey without you," he said. "I'll never be able to thank you enough."

"Oh, don't be silly." Callie smiled tremulously and gestured toward the porch where Peter was playing with the dogs. "We have Peter to thank, too. And everyone else."

"I know. And I won't ever forget that, Callie."

"Will Joey come back…?" She lowered her voice. "You know, to see Rebecca?"

He hesitated. "Things have a way of working out," he began, and then they were interrupted by Reese, who'd come by to let Mase know he'd be driving Berry down to Denver in the morning.

"Maybe I'll stop in at the trial," Reese said, "see how you're doing."

"I hope it's over pretty quick," Mase said. "And I'll have an answer for you soon, okay?"

Reese shook his hand. "Take your time, son," he said, and then he strode off toward the house.

"What was *that* all about?" Callie asked as Mase started the car.

"I'll tell you later," he said. He took her hand and squeezed it.

"Good luck at the trial," she said, not truly believing that he was going to drive off and she'd never see him again. There was so much she had to tell him, so many things…

"I'll call," Mase said, getting in the car.

She nodded, a lump forming in her throat, and then he and Joey were gone. If ever she needed a little magic, it was now.

CHAPTER EIGHTEEN

MASE MET RICHARD METCALF'S gaze for a moment before he turned his attention back to the man's lawyer and answered the question. "No, sir, I did not see Mr. Metcalf at Councilman Edwards's apartment."

Sleazebag smiled and nodded at the jury, then turned back to Mase, who'd been on the witness stand nearly the whole day. "So," the lawyer said, "my client cannot be placed at the crime scene?"

Mase looked at the man levelly. "That's correct, sir. Only Mr. Metcalf's employee can be placed at the murder scene."

"Objection!" Sleazebag barked, whirling toward the judge. "Your Honor, will you please instruct the witness to answer only the question posed to him?"

The judge turned toward Mase. "Detective, that is, Mr. LeBow, you must answer the question asked and not interject side comments. Is that understood?"

"Yes, sir," Mase said pleasantly.

The judge sighed and addressed the twelve jurors. "You are to disregard that last statement, ladies and gentlemen." Then to the court recorder, he added, "Strike Mr. LeBow's last reply."

Sleazebag frowned and went back to his cross-examination.

It was a game they all played, and Mase knew the rules. He pushed just so far and then politely backed off. The object of the game was simple: convey as much info to the jury as possible without appearing too strident or biased. Everyone in the courtroom—including the jurors—knew how the game was played, and thus far Mase was doing okay, across the fifty-yard line and sprinting toward the goal. The jury had already heard prosecution testimony that Richard Metcalf's voice had been identified as the one on the phone to Hank Berry, the voice giving explicit instructions to have the city councilman murdered. Mase had identified Berry as the man he'd bumped into at the crime scene, and things were looking bad for billionaire Metcalf.

Sleazebag posed another question to Mase. "All right, Mr. LeBow, let's move on to another subject. Did you drive to Mr. Metcalf's home and threaten him on the night of…"

Mase heard the question, and he answered honestly that he had indeed grabbed Metcalf and threatened him. Then Mase added, "Of course, he kidnapped my son, anyway."

"Objection!"

On it went. The game. Mase getting in his whole story despite the objections and terse warnings from the judge. The minutes ticked by, then hours. And while Sleazebag and the D.A. called out his rulings—often with a sidebar discussion—Mase couldn't help letting his thoughts drift.

Joey. Right now his grandparents were watching him down at Castle Pines, but school was going to start soon, and Mase had to come to a decision: put Joey in first grade here in Denver, or enroll him in Lightning Creek.

He thought about his last conversation with Reese

Hatcher before he and Joey had left for Denver. They'd been standing in the drive of the ranch.

"I'm gonna hang up the old hat next election," Reese had said. "The wife wants to spend the winters in the RV. Arizona, you know."

"Sounds nice," Mase had said.

"Well, anyway, Lightning Creek will be needing a new sheriff. Uh-huh. And I got to thinking about you, son, now that you've given up the Denver police."

Mase had been taken aback. "Me? What about your deputies? Shouldn't one of them run for the position?"

"'Fraid none of the boys wants the job. They all like the status quo. And that's when I got to thinking about you. Especially now that you and Miss Callie, well, you get my meaning."

Mase had said nothing. He got the meaning, all right, only too well. "What about the election? I mean, I'm not even a Wyoming resident."

But Reese had obviously thought that out. "No problem, son. You can establish residency in plenty of time to get your name on the ballot."

"Hmm," Mase had said. "That doesn't mean I'd win, Reese."

"Oh, you'll win. You'll be the only name *on* the ballot. Besides, you're a local hero."

"Me?"

"You betcha. Everybody in the county knows your whole life story."

"What?"

"Donna. My dispatcher."

"Oh," Mase had said. "Oh."

"So you just go on down to Denver and do your testifying, son, and think it over."

"Well…"

"Take your time. No rush." Then Reese had cast a sidelong glance at Callie, who stood talking with Joey and Rebecca. "Well, I wouldn't take *too* long, if you know what I mean. Miss Callie, she can be one impatient customer."

Mase had smiled and nodded and given her a look, too. Then he'd promised he'd think it over.

And he was. Right on the witness stand.

"What time did you arrive at Mr. Edwards's apartment?" Sleazebag was asking.

Mase replied. But it was getting harder and harder to concentrate. Hell, in the depositions he'd given, he'd answered these same questions so many times he'd lost count.

"It was dark by then," Sleazebag said. "How could you identify a face in the dark, Mr. LeBow?"

"The apartment complex is well-lit," Mase said, and he named the placement of all the lighting, and even the wattage of the bulbs for good measure.

Callie, he thought, trying not to let his concentration waver. Callie. If someone had told him last spring that he'd be bought at a bachelor auction and fall in love... Well, Mase would have said, "You're crazy."

Callie... With her whimsical expressions and her own special magic. And her horses. Subconsciously, he reached up and touched his brow, touched the red line where the rock had met his head when Diablo threw him. Maybe Callie wouldn't insist he ride again. Did a sheriff *have* to ride?

"Mr. LeBow, I'd like to ask you to explain to the jury, sir, why you quit the police force."

"Objection!" The D.A. leaped to his feet and the judge signaled the lawyers to his bench, where they began arguing in whispers.

What would Amy think? What would his late wife have told him to do? Mase thought hard about that, and the only thing he knew for sure was that she would have wanted Joey to have a family. Not just Mase and four grandparents, but a mother. And siblings. Amy had always wanted more children.

But did Callie?

Dumb question. Of course Callie would want kids. Probably dozens of them. Her own and every little lost soul she could get her hands on. She would put them on her horses, too, and let the magic begin. Oh, yeah.

Mase concentrated on the question being asked him. "...why you left the Denver police force?"

"Because I got sick of rich men like the defendant here getting away with murder. Literally."

Sleazebag's mouth dropped and the judge banged his gavel. "Mr. LeBow," the judge said in earnest, "I'll allow no more remarks like that in my courtroom. I promise, I will hold you in contempt if I hear anything more on those lines. Do you understand me?"

"Yes, sir," Mase said docilely, and out of the corner of his eye he saw a few of the jurors grinning. "I'm sorry, Your Honor."

Callie. Those big hazel eyes and fine golden hair. He saw her in his house in Denver, in his kitchen. He saw her mounting her horse, swinging that slim leg over the saddle horn. And he saw her in the barn, the dust motes dancing in the light, the hollow at the base of her throat, the firmness of her small breasts. God, how he wanted her.

But there was his house, his stuff—heck, he supposed he'd have a garage sale. A big one. And the things he needed, Joey's things... Put them all in a U-Haul and tow it to Wyoming. The house would sell quickly. He guessed he could rent a place in Lightning Creek. If Callie, well, if they got together, then she could choose where they'd live. He didn't care. The summer was tearing by and Joey would need to be in school. And Rebecca was in first grade, in Lightning Creek.

The judge called it a day at four-fifteen when Sleazebag said he had no more questions for Mason LeBow. The D.A. had hesitated, deciding whether or not to do a redirect examination, but apparently he was satisfied, and Mase was dismissed. He stepped down from the witness box and thought, *Free at last.* He couldn't believe how good he felt. He even smiled at Metcalf as he strode by. Not a malevolent smile, but a simple goodbye and good riddance. Then he was out of the courthouse, loosening his necktie and breathing in drafts of fresh air as he walked to his car.

What would his parents think if he told them he was moving to Wyoming? But Mase knew that answer. "Thank God," his mother would say, and his dad would pat him on the back. They already knew about Callie, thanks to Joey, who'd done nothing but talk about her and Rebecca and the ranch since they'd gotten back. It was as if the abduction had never happened. Someday Joey would understand. But for now he was talking about it as if it had been an adventure. A cold, wet one, but an adventure nonetheless.

He drove toward Castle Pines and thought a lot about Joey, and he knew that in the end, nothing was as important as his son's welfare.

Okay, Mase thought, what he felt about Callie was important, too. He loved her. There was no denying it or running from it. He loved her. And he was darn sure she loved him. Him and Joey. But would she marry him? They'd never talked about marriage. Hell, they'd never had time to even talk about love. So just where did that leave them?

He pulled up in front of his folks' place and parked, the questions still batting around his head. Then Joey banged open the front screen door and raced out to greet his father. Mase got out of the car and hugged him, tousled his hair, then waved at his mother, who was standing in the door, smiling.

Mase looked at his mother, he looked down at Joey and he knew. He supposed he'd known for a long time what he wanted and what he needed to do to get it. He put his hand on Joey's shoulder. "Hey, kiddo," he said, "you want to go for a walk, have a little man-to-man talk?"

Joey looked up. "What's a man-to-man talk, Daddy?"

Mase laughed and took his son's hand and began to walk down the sidewalk. "Well," he said, "it's like this. I've come to a decision. A real important decision, and I want to know how you feel about it."

Joey stopped and cocked his head. "You mean about moving to Wyoming?"

Magic, Mase thought. *There it was again.*

CALLIE FINISHED the chores early that day. She hardly knew what to do with herself now that summer was nearly gone and the ranch wasn't a three-ring circus anymore.

She perched on the top bar of the riding ring, boot heels hooked over the lower bar, chin resting on her fists, and ran her gaze over the ranch. It was quiet. The horses stood munching grain in the barn behind her. The cottonwoods surrounding the house looked a little tired, a little dirty. Before long the leaves would be turning, then falling, then it would snow.

Callie sighed. It had only been a few weeks, but Mase hadn't called and she missed him. She wondered how the trial was going, how Joey was doing.

Well, at least she had Saturday to look forward to, when the townsfolk would flock out to the ranch and there would be fun and gossip and therapy sessions.

She sat there and felt the breeze on her face. Her eyes strayed to the long ranch road. She couldn't help it; she had a nervous tic, watching the road for a dust plume and a blue Cherokee at the head of it. She squinted under the brim of her Stetson so she could see better, but there was no one on the road, no dust, no car. No Mase.

You've got to stop this, Thorne, she said to herself, and that's when the fantasy began.

She was sitting there on the fence, heels hooked to keep her balance, moping. Her eyes were fixed on the road, and suddenly she saw it, a dark dot turning in from the highway, a dark speck that got larger, and, yes, there was the dust cloud following it like the wake of a ship. She peered intently at it, her heart beating drumbeats in her chest. Was it…? Yes, it was his blue Cherokee!

Mase. Oh, my God, Mase was coming back!

Happiness overwhelmed her, a joy that brought tears to her eyes and a sweet warmth to her belly. Her life would be complete now. No matter what the future held, they'd be together, she and Mase. And Joey. Love swelled inside her like a beautiful flower unfolding to the sun.

She jumped down from the fence and ran to meet him. He stopped the car, and he and Joey piled out.

And there he was, right in front of her, close enough to touch, tall and handsome, his eyes a dark cobalt blue with emotion, and he was smiling at her. In a way he had never smiled before.

"Callie," he said.

"Mase?" she breathed.

"Callie, I'm here to stay. I love you."

"Oh, Mase." She ran to him and they threw their arms around each other. She could feel him, smell him. She was in his embrace, he loved her. Callie's life was complete. She was crying for joy, her face buried in his shoulder.

"I love you, too," she said.

He held her at arm's length and searched her face. "Will you marry me?" he asked in a smooth, deep voice that melted her insides.

"Yes," Callie whispered. "Yes, Mase, yes."

"Will you be my mother now?" came Joey's piping voice.

"Yes, pardner, I will."

They clung to each other and Joey, too. The sun was shining on the Someday Ranch. The horses whinnied with happiness. Beavis and Butt-Head galloped over to jump and whine with delight. Even the barn cats came out and twined around their ankles, purring. Birds sang overhead.

Oh, come on, Callie thought, ending the dream. *You overdid it this time.*

She sighed again, unhooking her heels from the fence, and started to climb down. She would go inside, shower, help Francine with dinner. Not that Francine needed much help these days, what with the paltry crew that was left, Callie thought, glancing toward the house. And that's when she saw the dark speck turn onto the ranch road.

She stopped short and peered beneath her hat brim. She closed her eyes tight and opened them again. It was still there.

She put a hand on top of her hat to hold it on and gave her head a shake.

It was *still* there, growing larger by the second. A blue Cherokee with a plume of dust billowing in its wake.

"Oh," Callie whispered, but she didn't run to meet him as she had in her fantasy; she was frozen to the spot, couldn't move a muscle.

The car pulled up, the doors opened, Mase and Joey got out. Her heart stopped then, just skipped a whole beat, then began a new, heavy rhythm.

Mase looked around, took off his sunglasses in the slow, macho, seductive way he had. Still she couldn't move. He spotted her, but he didn't smile, not as he had in the fantasy. He looked at her, seriously, meaningfully.

"Callie," he said.

"Mase?" she breathed.

It didn't happen exactly as it had in her fantasy. It wasn't nearly as easy.

"I'm back," he told her.

"So I see."

"I'm going to run for sheriff."

"You are?"

"I have to establish residence in Wyoming, so I..."

"And that's why you've come back. Of course." *So much for fantasies.*

"But I..." He took a deep breath. "I thought we might... I thought maybe we could...see each other."

"Sure we can see each other. Well, heck, Mase, I can see you right now."

He frowned. "I meant, we could see each other a lot."

"A lot?"

"Damn it, Callie, I mean I'm crazy about you, and I want you to marry me." He sounded angry.

"Really?"

"Yes, really. Stop it, Callie, you're driving me nuts."

"Well, I love you, too."

"Really?"

"Hey, that's *my* line."

"God, Callie."

Her muscles finally overcame their paralysis, and she hopped down from the fence and grinned.

"Okay," she said.

"Okay what?"

"I'll marry you." She took her hat off and slapped it against her thigh. "But you have to promise one thing."

"What one thing?"

"You won't give me speeding tickets when you're sheriff."

"Aw, Callie, Reese already told me that." Then he took her in his arms and kissed her, and Joey giggled, and somewhere a horse whinnied, loudly and triumphantly.

"I guess it's okay with everyone," she gasped.

"It better be," he said, and he bent his head to kiss her again.

continues with

BACHELOR FATHER

by Vicki Lewis Thompson

New York fashion editor Katherine Seymour had thought
a three-day retreat in Yellowstone would be just the thing
to get her life back on track. But she hadn't planned on
slipping into a rushing river...or being saved by a very
sexy Ranger.

When Katherine learned of the Bachelor Auction almost
a year later, she knew what she had to do. Make the
highest bid...and introduce Zeke Lonetree to
his daughter.

Available in September
Here's a preview!

"CLOSE THE DOOR gently if you can, so you don't startle her."

Zeke glanced at Katherine and caught his breath. Her green blouse was unfastened, although she'd modestly pulled it around her so that her breast barely showed. Somehow that made the picture more erotic to Zeke. Rain drummed on the roof of the truck, but he could still hear the soft sucking noises Amanda made while she nursed.

He pulled the door closed as best he could, knowing he'd have to open it and slam it again before they started driving. Then he stared straight ahead and tried to concentrate on following the path of an individual raindrop as it slid down the windshield. He seemed to be having trouble getting enough air, and he cracked his window open a little.

A woman nursing her child was no big deal, he told himself. He lived among wild animals who raised their young that way, and this was the same thing. Except it wasn't even close. A year ago, he'd desperately wanted this woman, and she'd desperately wanted him. Now, the result of their mating that night lay in her arms, the tiny mouth fastened to her breast. God help him, he wanted this woman still.

"There's no way to fix the tire, is there?" Katherine asked quietly.

"No." He cleared the hoarseness from his throat, hoping she didn't notice. He didn't want her to know how she still affected him.

"Maybe someone will come along."

"That's not likely." He took a deep breath and let it out. "We're going to have to drive with the tire flat. I have a cabin out here. It's not far. From there we can call a tow truck."

"You live out here?"

"Yeah, when I'm not on duty at the park. It beats renting an apartment somewhere."

She nodded. "I can't picture you in an apartment. I imagine you clearing the land and building something out of logs, like Daniel Boone or Davy Crockett."

Zeke grinned. "Which is exactly what I did."

Katherine gazed at him, her expression wistful. "That's the first time you've smiled since we met at the lodge."

"Yeah, well, this experience hasn't been a laugh a minute," Zeke said wryly.

"But Amanda is such a beautiful little girl. I wish you could share some of the joy I feel."

"You're really happy about this?" he asked.

"How could I help being happy? Maybe I was a bit shocked when the doctor told me I was pregnant, but in about five minutes the shock wore off and I started feeling excited. A new life was growing inside me. That's a miraculous thing, Zeke."

He wondered if he'd have reacted that positively if she'd called to tell him right away. Maybe not, but he'd never know. Well-meaning though she might have been, she'd cheated him out of that sense of anticipation.

Katherine made a slight turn toward him, tempting

him again with the perfect picture of motherhood she represented. ''My only regret is whatever trouble I'm causing you.''

Zeke looked away, breaking eye contact. ''You haven't caused me any trouble,'' he said. *''Yet.''*

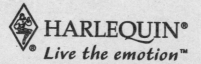

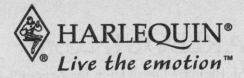
HARLEQUIN®
Live the emotion™

eHARLEQUIN.com

The Ultimate Destination for Women's Fiction

Visit eHarlequin.com's Bookstore today for today's most popular books at great prices.

- An extensive selection of romance books by top authors!

- Choose our convenient "bill me" option. No credit card required.

- New releases, Themed Collections and hard-to-find backlist.

- A sneak peek at upcoming books.

- Check out book excerpts, book summaries and Reader Recommendations from other members and post your own too.

- Find out what everybody's reading in Bestsellers.

- Save BIG with everyday discounts and exclusive online offers!

- Our Category Legend will help you select reading that's exactly right for you!

- Visit our Bargain Outlet often for huge savings and special offers!

- Sweepstakes offers. Enter for your chance to win special prizes, autographed books and more.

Your purchases are 100% guaranteed—so shop online at www.eHarlequin.com today!

HARLEQUIN®
Presents

The world's bestselling romance series...
The series that brings you your favorite authors,
month after month:

Helen Bianchin...Emma Darcy
Lynne Graham...Penny Jordan
Miranda Lee...Sandra Marton
Anne Mather...Carole Mortimer
Susan Napier...Michelle Reid

and many more uniquely talented authors!

Wealthy, powerful, gorgeous men...
Women who have feelings just like your own...
The stories you love, set in exotic, glamorous locations...

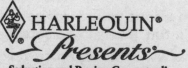

HARLEQUIN®
Presents

Seduction and Passion Guaranteed!

HPDIR104